IS THE DERBY WORTH LOSING
THE PEOPLE YOU CARE ABOUT?

"Who cares about the naysayers?" Reaching up, she stroked Image. "*We* know Image can handle the Derby. It's . . ." She hesitated, a lump rising in her throat.

"It's Ashleigh and Mike, right?" Jazz said softly.

Melanie's lower lip trembled. "And Christina and Cindy and Ben and Ian. If we race Image in the Derby, we're racing against my family, my *friends*. At first I thought it would be okay. But now I can feel them looking at me and Image like we're definite rivals."

"So that's what you meant earlier," Jazz said. "About things changing when you got back from Florida."

Melanie nodded. "And don't say I'm imagining it. Cindy and Ben were at the paddock before today's race, and it wasn't to cheer me on. And I hated to hear Janice Hart say it, but she was right—Ashleigh and Mike *weren't* at the winner's circle today, because they *are* upset. Ashleigh and Christina have *huge* hopes for Star—Triple Crown hopes—and I think that mock race when Image almost beat Star scared the heck out of them.

"If we enter Image in the Derby, I'm afraid I'll lose them, Jazz," Melanie added miserably. "And I'm not sure one race is worth the risk."

Collect all the books in the Thoroughbred series

Collect all the books in the Ashleigh series

*coming soon

THOROUGHBRED

FAITH IN A LONG SHOT

CREATED BY

JOANNA CAMPBELL

WRITTEN BY

ALICE LEONHARDT

HarperEntertainment
An Imprint of HarperCollinsPublishers

🏰 HarperEntertainment
An Imprint of HarperCollins*Publishers*
10 East 53rd Street, New York, NY 10022-5299

Produced by 17th Street Productions, an Alloy Online, Inc., company

HarperCollins books are available at special quantity discounts for bulk purchases for sales promotions, premiums, or fund-raising. For information please call or write: Special Markets Department, HarperCollins Publishers Inc., 10 East 53rd Street, New York, NY 10022-5299. Telephone: (212) 207-7528. Fax: (212) 207-7222.

ISBN 0-06-009049-9

First printing: February 2003

Printed in the United States of America

Visit HarperEntertainment on the World Wide Web at
www.harpercollins.com

❖ 10 9 8 7 6 5 4 3

THE BLACK FILLY REARED, HER FRONT LEGS STRIKING AT THE cloudless spring sky as if it were an enemy. Her coat gleamed like the finest silk; the muscles in her flanks rippled with strength. Foam flew from her mouth, and her nostrils flared as if she'd been galloping for miles. Tossing her mane, the filly neighed a challenge, then leaped forward, her hooves slicing deep into the soft earth.

"Image, quit the theatrics!" Melanie Graham exclaimed as she held tightly to the end of the filly's lead line. "This isn't a scene from *Black Beauty*. All I want you to do is load in that trailer!"

Behind Melanie, Jazz Taylor chuckled. He was standing by the open trailer door holding a carrot, which Image had been ignoring for the past half hour.

Melanie shot Jazz an exasperated look as Image

dragged her away from the trailer ramp. "Don't encourage her tantrums, Jazz," she huffed. "This is *your* fault. You wanted her fit and ready for today's race. Well, she's so darn full of herself, we may never get her to Keeneland!"

"I told you what you needed to do," Jazz said as he took a bite of carrot. "You're just too stubborn to listen to *my* advice."

Melanie rolled her eyes. Pulling on the lead rope, she got Image turned in a circle. The three-year-old was so strong, Melanie knew she couldn't overpower her. But outsmarting Image was also getting harder. The filly had a mind of her own and knew how to use it to get her way. It was Image's intelligence and spirit that had attracted Melanie to her in the first place, but those qualities were proving to be a double-edged sword. They had helped Image come in second in the Florida Derby against colts. But they had also made training and handling her a daily challenge.

"Jazz, I know you're Image's owner," Melanie said as she steered the filly back toward the trailer. "But I'm her trainer. So let me handle this."

Jazz shrugged. "Okay, but when you change your mind and decide to follow my suggestion, just let me know." Smiling roguishly, he bit off another chunk of carrot and began to chew.

Melanie brushed her blond bangs from her damp brow and sighed. *How could one guy be so sure of himself and look so adorable at the same time?* Jazz wore faded jeans slung low on his hips and a baggy black T-shirt. His dark hair was held back in a ponytail. He was the lead singer in the popular band Pegasus, and whenever he went to the track with Melanie, he dressed down. Otherwise autograph seekers and fans mobbed him. But no matter how he was dressed, he looked great to Melanie. They'd gotten to know each other over the past six months, and Melanie's feelings had grown more and more complicated. She couldn't deny her attraction to him, yet she knew there was no way they could have a relationship. Not only was he her boss in a sense, but he traveled constantly with the band. He'd flown in for that day's race, but Melanie had no idea how long he'd stay. Hardly great conditions for a romance.

With another sigh, Melanie shook any lingering thoughts of Jazz from her head. Image could sense when Melanie wasn't paying total attention to her, and that was probably one reason the filly wasn't cooperating. Melanie knew she had better focus. That afternoon Image was racing in the Ashland Stakes at Keeneland. The race would test her speed against top fillies from all over the United States. The outcome of the race would also tell Jazz and Melanie whether they'd made the right decision about Image's future.

But we have to get her to Keeneland first! Melanie reminded herself as she again led the filly toward the trailer ramp. Usually patience, coaxing, and carrots won out. But that morning Image was especially interested in playing games rather than cooperating.

"What was that advice again, Jazz?" Melanie tried not to sound peevish as Image once again planted her hooves at the end of the ramp and refused to budge. Saturday morning was so busy at Whitebrook that she didn't dare ask Jonnie or Dani for help. But she also hated to admit that Jazz might be right.

"Load Baby in the van and take her to the track with Image," Jazz said with a grin. Baby was a shaggy pony that Image had been stabled with in Florida. When Image had refused to go back to Kentucky without her, Jazz bought Baby from her owner. Melanie had to admit that having Baby along had made the ride home a lot more peaceful than the ride from Kentucky to Florida.

"But I'm trying to wean Image off Baby," Melanie protested. "It's bad enough that we have to van Image everywhere because she's too spoiled to stay in a racetrack stall. Now we have to bring her buddy with her, too?"

Jazz chuckled. "Looks that way. Just call her Diva from now on."

Melanie blew out a frustrated breath. Ears pricked, Image stared at her as if she knew they were discussing her antics. Then she threw her head around, gazed in the direction of the Whitebrook barns, and whickered longingly. A shrill, plaintive nicker rang back.

"Oh, all right." Melanie knew when she was beaten. "Get Baby. At least she's easier to cart around than Pirate."

Jazz whooped. "Yes! Give me five, Image," he said, holding out his hand. "We won." Image bumped his palm with her muzzle, and Jazz shot Melanie a victorious smile before jogging toward the barn.

While she waited for Baby, Melanie led Image to a patch of grass. Dropping her head, the filly began to graze. Melanie readjusted Image's shipping boots, then leaned against the filly's side and laced her fingers through the soft black mane. The morning sun was rising above the barn roofs, bathing Whitebrook in a golden glow. Ashleigh Griffen and Mike Reese, Melanie's aunt and uncle, owned the Kentucky Thoroughbred farm where Melanie kept Image. Melanie had lived there with her aunt and uncle ever since she was twelve. Her dad, Will Graham, and stepmother, Susan, were busy running Graham Productions in New York City. At first, living at Whitebrook had been tough on Melanie. She had missed her dad and her old life in the city. But then she'd gotten hooked on Thoroughbreds and racing, and she'd never looked back.

It was early Saturday morning, and several exercise riders were jogging horses around the oval training track. Melanie caught sight of her cousin Christina's blue-and-white helmet cover. She was trotting Wonder's Star, her handsome chestnut colt, along the outside railing. When Melanie had first arrived at Whitebrook, she and her cousin had clashed. Now they were best friends.

At least we used to be best friends, Melanie thought sadly. Lately they hadn't been spending much time together. Christina was busy with Star, and Melanie was busy with Image. Except for the brief daily rides to and from Henry Clay High School, where they both were seniors, they barely had time to talk anymore. Although that wasn't the only reason they'd been avoiding each other, Melanie knew. Melanie had been furious with her cousin after Christina had crashed in a race on Raven, one of Melanie's favorite horses. Fortunately, Raven's tendons were healing, although the filly would never race again. Melanie had tried to forgive her cousin—accidents did happen—but deep down part of her still blamed Christina for not paying enough attention during the race.

All Christina thinks about is Star, Star, Star, Melanie thought as she patted Image's shoulder. Melanie figured that was where her cousin's mind had been during Raven's race. The duo had recently returned from California. Now Christina was getting Star fit and ready for the Kentucky Derby, which was the first Saturday in May. Ashleigh had insisted that Star take it slow and easy. She wanted the colt to be able to handle the grueling Triple Crown. She'd also insisted that Chris get in as much racing as possible to get ready to ride against top jockeys in the Derby. So that day Chris was riding Rascal, Fast Gun, and Catwink, who were already at Keeneland. Ashleigh and Mike were there as well, getting their horses—and clients' horses—ready. Because Image hated to be confined in a stall, Melanie had waited until the last minute to van her to the track. That meant they had to hurry.

Melanie glanced impatiently toward the barn. *What's taking Jazz so long?* Baby was hardly difficult to control.

Joe Kisner, who usually hauled the horses, was at Keeneland with the others, so Melanie was driving the truck and trailer. She didn't want to have to rush. The Ashland Stakes was an important race for Image. The Grade I, 1 $\frac{1}{16}$-mile race attracted stakes-winning fillies from all over. Glitter and Take Charge had arrived from the West Coast. The East Coast fillies Blushing Bride, who had won the Bonnie Miss, and Wave Dancer, winner of the Fair Ground Oaks, were also entered. Many of the fillies who did well in the Ashland Stakes would go on to race in the prestigious Kentucky Oaks, the filly equivalent of the Kentucky Derby. But if Image did well, Melanie and Jazz had bigger—and riskier—plans.

So far, Image and Glitter, who'd won the Santa Anita Oaks, were favored in the Ashland Stakes. Melanie knew that Image had the talent and the heart to win—but she also knew that in horse racing there

7

were no guarantees. And with a filly as unpredictable as Image, Melanie had learned there were *definitely* no guarantees.

"Diva is the perfect nickname for you," Melanie said as she stroked Image's sleek neck. Head up, the filly was staring intently in the direction of the barn. Blades of grass hung from her lips. When she spotted Jazz and Baby, she twirled sideways. Melanie, who'd been relaxing against the filly's shoulder, lost her balance and fell awkwardly under the horse's dancing hooves. Image pranced around Melanie, careful not to step on her. Flushing with embarrassment, Melanie scrambled to her feet. "Whoa!" She tugged angrily on the lead, although she knew it was her own fault she'd almost gotten trampled. Daydreaming around a Thoroughbred was a recipe for disaster.

When Image finally halted, Melanie glanced over at Jazz. He was pressing his lips together, trying not to chuckle. "Oh, go ahead and laugh," Melanie snapped, still angry at her carelessness. Image could have easily ripped the lead line from her hand and romped madly around the farm, tearing a tendon or crashing into something. It wouldn't have been the first time she'd gotten loose.

"You have to admit that was pretty funny," Jazz said with a grin as he led Baby up. Image touched noses with the fuzzy pony, and the two whuffed excitedly.

Melanie shook her head. "You'd think they'd been apart for weeks instead of a few minutes."

"They miss each other," Jazz said softly, his dark eyes on Melanie. She blushed. Was Jazz saying he'd missed *her?*

No way. Melanie instantly dismissed the idea. When Pegasus was on tour, female fans swarmed the members of the band. Jazz could have any girl he wanted, whenever he wanted.

"Hurry and load Baby in the front," Melanie said brusquely, trying to hide her mixed-up emotions.

Jazz led Baby to the trailer's side door. In Florida, they'd discovered the tiny pony fit perfectly in the front compartment. When Baby calmly stepped into the trailer, Melanie led Image toward the ramp. The filly scrambled inside, practically loading herself. Melanie blew out a breath of relief. One crisis averted. How many more would there be before the afternoon's race?

With Jazz's help, Melanie raised the ramp and secured the doors. Then she checked and rechecked the latches, trailer hitch, tires, supplies—*everything.* Since she was driving, she wanted to be doubly careful.

"Ready?" Jazz asked.

Frowning, she kicked the back right trailer tire. "Does that look low to you?"

"No, Melanie. Everything is fine. You sure you don't want me to drive?" Jazz looked concerned.

A few weeks before, Melanie had wrecked the Blazer she shared with Christina. *Not that it was my fault,* she reminded herself. *"You* driving a truck and trailer? Now *that* would be scary," Melanie joked as she strode to the driver's side.

Minutes later, the truck was crawling down the driveway, the trailer rattling behind. Jazz looked at his watch. "Let's see. At ten miles per hour, we'll reach Keeneland about the same time Glitter crosses the finish line to win the Ashland Stakes."

Melanie reached over and slapped him on the shoulder. "No way. Image will be there. And she'll win. We have plenty of time."

At the end of the drive onto the road, Melanie checked each way before slowly pulling out. Jazz stared at her.

"Are you sure you've driven this rig before?" he asked.

"I've been practicing. Lots. But I admit this is the first time I've driven without Joe or Mike."

Jazz made a strangling sound. "We're going to die!"

"Oh, shut up." Melanie punched him playfully on the shoulder. But inside, her stomach was churning.

Jazz turned in the passenger seat to face her. "Um, Melanie, seriously, I heard Mike offer to come back and drive Image. Why didn't you say yes? Riding Image in the race will be exhausting enough. I know you're Wonder Woman, but you don't need to do everything."

Melanie bit her bottom lip. As she drove down the road, her eyes kept darting from the rearview mirror to the side mirror to the road. "I'm not sure why I did that," she said, but even she could hear the lie in her voice.

Jazz frowned. "Is something going on I don't know about?"

Melanie clenched the steering wheel tightly. "I'm not sure anything's going on. But ever since I came back from Florida, things have been different." She cast a sideways glance at him. He was listening intently, his eyes on her face. "Only I don't *think* it had anything to do with Florida. I think it has to do with . . ." Melanie wrinkled her nose, trying to figure out what she was trying to say. If she had asked Ashleigh or Mike or Chris if things had changed, they would have replied with an emphatic no. But ever since she'd come back from Florida, things had changed. And not just because of Christina and Raven. Melanie had noticed *something*. She wasn't quite sure what to call it—it was like a slight chilliness or politeness whenever she was around the family.

"Look, I can't talk about it right now," Melanie said quickly. "The highway's up ahead. You've got to help me with road signs. And I've got to concentrate. That's precious cargo back there."

Jazz nodded in agreement. "But if there's something bothering you, Mel, we need to talk."

"I agree." Melanie felt a warm rush. When they were together in Florida, she'd gradually come to realize how much she relied on Jazz's friendship and support. At first she'd been horrified when she found out he was going to be Image's sole owner. Racing Image was a dream come true for her, and she didn't want anyone else telling her what to do. But she soon found out that training and racing the filly required numerous decisions. Now, in more ways than Melanie could count, she was glad that Jazz was there to help.

"This race is really important," he reminded her. "Especially if we're entering Image in the Kentucky Derby."

The Kentucky Derby. Ever since they'd found out that Image could hold her own against colts, Melanie and Jazz had talked about running her in the Kentucky Derby. They'd even announced it to the world. Except now that the race was getting close, Melanie was plagued with serious doubts. The Derby was not only the first jewel of the Triple Crown, it was considered one of the premier races in the world. Melanie knew that Jazz had high hopes for Image. But winning one race against colts did not mean that Image could take on the world's best three-year-olds. Image was a powerful runner. But she was also a filly. Only three fillies in history had ever won the Kentucky Derby. No matter how confident Melanie had been acting, deep down inside, she was seriously worried that entering Image in the Derby was a huge mistake. She just hadn't admitted it to Jazz.

"You need to focus on Image," Jazz continued as he fiddled with the truck's radio, "not problems at home. It would be a shame to miss a shot at the Derby because you were worried about nothing."

Melanie didn't need to be reminded. The night before, she'd spent hours studying the program for that day's race, which listed all the horses and their statistics. Unlike Jazz, Melanie wasn't worried just about a shot at the Derby. She was also worried about the Ashland Stakes. When she'd finally turned out the light, visions of Glitter and Wave Dancer bursting across the finish line wouldn't leave her mind. The fillies were both strong, and there was a good possibility that either one could beat Image—especially if Melanie lost her focus or if Image pulled one of her stunts. And if Image couldn't cut it in the Ashland, she'd never make it in the Kentucky Derby.

Melanie looked sideways at Jazz. A popular song had come on the radio, and he was tapping a beat on his leg. As much as he worried about Image, Melanie knew the filly wasn't the most important thing in his life. But Image *was* the most important thing in hers.

So many things could happen during a race, and she didn't think there was any way she'd risk her beloved filly—even for the Kentucky Derby. If Image didn't win that day, Mel decided, she would tell Jazz how she felt. Even if it meant sacrificing their Derby dream.

2

AN HOUR LATER MELANIE PULLED THE RIG INTO KEENE-
land's back side and parked in front of Barn 32, situ-
ated close to the training track. Immediately Ashleigh
came out of a stall. When Melanie shut off the truck
motor, Jazz called hello and climbed out to meet her.
Melanie sat frozen in the seat. Her fingers were clutch-
ing the steering wheel so tightly they ached. Visions of
the Kentucky Derby and the Ashland Stakes whirled
in her head.

You should have accepted Mike's offer, Melanie told
herself. Driving the rig had been nerve-racking, especially on the highway. She gently rubbed the left side of
her ribs, which were still slightly sore from the accident
with the Blazer. Then she checked her watch. In an hour
she had to be in the jockeys' lounge. That gave her

enough time to settle Image . . . *if* the filly cooperated.

Ashleigh rapped on the window. "Mel? You okay? We were worried when it took you guys so long to get here."

Melanie nodded. Turning, she smiled at her aunt, but Ashleigh was walking to the back of the trailer to help Joe unload Image. Melanie opened the truck door and climbed out. Neither Joe nor Ashleigh said a word to her until Image backed down the ramp.

"She looks good," Ashleigh said. "Put her in stall six," she added before heading back to the stall she'd come out of. At the sound of Ashleigh's footsteps a horse hung its head over the stall guard, and Melanie recognized Catwink.

Was Melanie imagining things, or had Ashleigh seemed abrupt?

While Melanie cleaned the manure from the trailer, Joe led Image around the paddock area between the two barns, letting her stretch her legs. The filly danced on the end of the lead, her eyes flashing as she took in the sights. Melanie noticed the grooms at Barn 31 stop their chores to stare. And no wonder—Image had a regal presence that practically shouted, *Look at me! I'm so special!*

Jazz came around to the back of the trailer, Baby following alongside. "Ashleigh's right, she does look good," he said, grinning proudly. "Like a winner."

"If you say *winner* one more time, I'll whack you

with this." Melanie raised the rake threateningly. "I'm nervous enough. Why don't you let Baby stretch her legs, too?"

While Jazz led Baby around the barns, Melanie finished cleaning the trailer, then began unloading her supplies. She pulled out her jockey bag and saddle and set them on the ground. Then she went over to take off Image's wraps.

"Boy, I should have accepted Mike's offer to drive the rig," she said to Joe as she walked toward him.

"Rough ride?" He halted Image, who butted him fondly. Not only had Joe hauled Image to Florida, he'd been invaluable the week they were there.

"No, Image was fine." Melanie stooped next to the filly's front leg. "It's driving on the highway that's stressful." Pausing, she glanced at Catwink's stall. "Um, speaking of stress . . . is Ashleigh okay? She seemed, well, *tense*."

Joe shrugged. "Prerace jitters," he said, but when he wouldn't meet Melanie's eyes, she knew there was something more.

Standing, she faced him. "What's going on?"

He cast a quick glance at the barn, then said in a low voice, "Ashleigh's upset because Mike decided not to run Catwink in the Ashland Stakes."

Melanie blinked in surprise. "I didn't even know she'd been nominated for the race."

17

"She was nominated, all right. But after Image beat Catwink soundly in that mock race you guys rode, Mike decided he didn't want to chance a Whitebrook horse losing to Image."

A shiver ran up Melanie's spine. Bending, she busied herself with Image's other shipping boot. Mike had called Catwink a Whitebrook horse. That meant that even though Melanie dressed in the Whitebrook colors, Mike and Ashleigh didn't think of Image as a Whitebrook horse. They thought of her as a rival.

"So Mike pulled her," Joe added. "She's running in a claiming race instead. I think they're worried they'll lose her."

"Why'd they have to put her in a claiming race?" Melanie asked. "Couldn't they have entered her in an allowance race?" At all tracks, claiming races were common, and every trainer and owner ran horses in them. Before each meet, trainers carefully decided which races would be best for their horses. They could enter their horses in an allowance, handicap, stakes, or maiden race. Catwink couldn't enter maiden races because they were only for horses that had never won. In allowance and handicap races, certain weights were assigned to each horse. In a claiming race, someone could put a claim certificate on Catwink before the race. That meant the person could purchase Catwink for the claim amount after the race, whether she won or lost. Melanie knew that Ashleigh and Mike would

18

enter Catwink in the claiming race only if they felt she had the best chance of doing well.

"I guess Catwink didn't qualify for the allowance race, and she needed to run this weekend," Joe replied.

"Oh." Melanie wasn't quite sure what to say. So she hadn't been imagining Ashleigh's coolness.

Melanie loved her aunt and uncle. They'd been supportive through all her ups and downs. She'd *never* intentionally hurt them. But she also knew there were times when Image would compete against one of their horses. *Like in the Kentucky Derby.*

Melanie bit her lip as she walked around Image's rump to pull off the last boot. *What a mess!* Then Melanie told herself there was nothing she could do about it now. *This time the damage is done.*

When the wraps were off, Joe led Image toward her stall. The filly balked, then, like a little kid throwing a tantrum, reared and flung herself sideways. Joe deftly moved with her until she halted, trembling, a frantic expression in her dark eyes. Swinging her head around, she whinnied for Baby.

"We're in here," Jazz called from Image's stall. Image lunged toward them, dragging Joe with her.

Melanie rubbed her temples. She hoped this feistiness wasn't a foretaste of Image's behavior during the race.

When Image was in the stall, Jazz scooted out, dragging Baby with him. Joe unhooked the lead line and hurried out, too. Immediately Image began striking the door with her hoof until Baby was tied and settled under her nose.

"Crisis number two handled," Melanie muttered to herself. Then she picked up her bag and saddle. "If you two are okay, I'm heading to the jockeys' lounge."

"We're fine," Jazz replied. "And don't worry about Image. I've got her under control."

Melanie laughed. Image was biting at the stall door as if trying to tear it down. "I can see that."

"Wait, Mel," Jazz called as she turned to leave. In two strides he was in front of her. Smiling tenderly, he touched her on the cheek. Melanie caught her breath. *Is he going to give me a kiss for good luck?* Her body flushed with anticipation, but he just said, "See you in the paddock."

"Oh, right." Melanie gulped and spun around. Cheeks red, she hurried off. *Jeez, Graham, what a dope you are!*

As she passed Catwink's stall, Melanie slowed and glanced inside. Ashleigh was bent over, wrapping the filly's legs. Catwink was a sixteen-hand gray filly with a sleek build. *Like a greyhound*, Melanie thought. She *was* fast, but Image, who was sixteen two hands and built like a colt, had outpowered her in the mock race.

"Hi, Aunt Ashleigh. Good luck," she called into the stall.

Ashleigh didn't even look up. "Thanks. We'll need it."

Melanie opened her mouth, wanting to say that she understood why Ashleigh was miffed and that she was sorry they had to enter their filly in a claiming race. Catwink was one of Mike and Ashleigh's favorites, and she knew they didn't want to lose her. But she was afraid she'd only make things worse.

"Anything you want me to tell Christina?" she asked instead.

"Nope. We'll see her in the paddock. Thanks anyway." Tilting her head up, Ashleigh flashed her a brief smile before moving to Catwink's back leg. Melanie hoped Ashleigh's smile meant that her aunt was upset not at her but with the situation.

When Melanie reached the jockeys' lounge, it was buzzing with activity. She waved to Karen Groves and Fred Anderson, calling congratulations to Fred, who had recently won his forty-fifth race and turned from bug to journeyman jockey. She nodded to the regulars, including Sammy Fingers and George Valdez, who rode strictly on the tracks in Kentucky. And she curiously eyeballed the half-dozen top-name jockeys who'd flown into Lexington for the Ashland Stakes.

Christina was already in the women's locker room, dressing in Whitebrook silks. Since she was riding in the first race, she needed to be ready early. "Hey, cuz,"

Melanie greeted as she opened her locker. "There're some big guns out there."

"Yeah, but they're not going to bother me," Christina said as she slid her boots from her carry bag. "I'm not riding in a prestigious race like the Ashland Stakes. Remember?"

"Um, right." Melanie frowned. *Is that a dig?* she wondered. "I know you're riding Catwink in the fifth race. Who else?"

"Rascal in the first. Fast Gun in the seventh." Christina sat down on a bench and pulled on her boots.

"Busy, busy. Be careful on Fast Gun."

Christina gave her a cool look. "Thanks for the warning, but I think I can handle him." She stood up. "Well, gotta get weighed in." Picking up her saddle, she headed out.

"Good luck," Melanie called after her. Then she shivered. If Christina had been any chillier, Melanie would have gotten frostbite.

Melanie thought back to the mock race when Image and Melanie had raced against Christina on Star and Dani on Catwink. It had been only six furlongs, and Star and Image had crossed the finish line nose to nose. Later Melanie and Christina had joked about sharing the winner's circle at the Derby. Looking back, Melanie realized the joking had sounded pretty forced. No one really wanted to share such an important win.

Still, Melanie vowed to have a heart-to-heart talk with her cousin. Somehow she had to make Christina understand that being rivals on occasion didn't have to change their relationship. At least it didn't change the way Melanie felt about Christina.

Heaving a big sigh, Melanie zipped open her bag. Racing Thoroughbreds was tough enough. She didn't need to add the risk of ruining relationships to her worries.

"Don't forget to rate her for the first part of the race," Jazz instructed Melanie as he gave her a leg up onto Image. They were standing outside the number seven saddling stall in Keeneland's paddock, located behind the grandstand. Trying not to attract attention, Jazz had put on sunglasses and stuck his signature long hair under a baseball cap. "Then let her go at the three-eighths pole for the last furlong," he continued solemnly. "Only don't get so far behind that she can't catch up."

Melanie gathered her reins, then glanced down at him. "Do you even know what you're talking about, Jazz?" she teased, though her stomach felt tied in knots.

"No. But it sounded good." He laughed nervously. "And we need some kind of plan. This is an impressive field."

Melanie was glad she wasn't the only one who was

anxious about the race. Before the paddock judge had announced riders up, she'd had a chance to study the other fillies. And Jazz was right—it *was* an impressive field. All the fillies were winners of major races. All were powerful and fit. In fact, the *only* thing that distinguished Image from the others was that she didn't have a big-name jockey on board. Definitely *not* a plus in a stakes race.

Melanie grabbed a hunk of mane as she searched for her short stirrups. Image had a hump in her back, and Melanie didn't want to get bounced from the saddle. The filly was already jigging in place, eager to get moving. As they headed from the paddock to the walking ring, Jazz jiggled the lead clipped to Image's bit, trying to keep her attention.

The crowd of people clustered around the rail was noisily pointing and gawking at the seven entries. Copies of the *Daily Racing Form* in hand, they checked each filly as she walked by. In a few minutes, many would rush back into the clubhouse to place their bets.

Melanie glanced up at the tote board. Image's odds had started out at 10 to 1. Now they were 8 to 5. Melanie figured that meant the crowd liked what they saw. *And what's not to like?* Image felt good—great, actually. As soon as Jazz led the filly into the paddock, Melanie could tell that Image knew why she was at Keeneland. Her stride was long, her neck arched, her eye keen. There was no whinnying for Baby or balking at the gate. Image was there to win.

While they walked around the ring, Jazz kept up a stream of nervous chatter. Melanie nodded as if listening, but her mind was on the other horses and jockeys. *I wish Mike were walking me around the ring.* It wasn't that she didn't like being with Jazz, but her uncle could quickly size up the other horses and riders. As she studied the entries, Melanie thought about each filly's statistics and tried to guess what Mike would say. *Watch out for the number one horse, Glitter, with Tommy Turner on board. She's a West Coast stakes winner with an experienced jockey. Don't worry about the number two filly, Take Charge—she'll burn out before the first mile. Keep your eye on Vicky Frontiere and Blushing Bride, the winner of the Bonnie Miss. Wave Dancer, number four, won the Fair Oaks. The jockey's some hotshot flown in from California, which means the owner thinks she can win. Number six, Golden Idol, hasn't done much, but her timed works were fast. And number seven, Incredible, has three wins under her belt. She also has Steve Quinn on board. And you know Steve. He's one of the best.*

Melanie gulped. With the back of one hand, she wiped the sweat trickling from under her helmet. Instead of helping, her inner monologue had made things worse.

Jazz halted Image beside the gate that led into the

tunnel under Keeneland's clubhouse. Melanie scanned the crowd around the walking ring. Had Ashleigh or Mike stopped by to wish her luck? She didn't see either, but she spotted Cindy McLean and Ben al-Rihani looking intently at their race programs. Ben was the owner of Tall Oaks Farm. Cindy managed the farm and trained the horses. Together they owned the stallion Champion, and Ben owned Gratis, a fast but hard-to-handle three-year-old colt also slated for the Kentucky Derby. *What are they doing here?* Melanie wondered. She hadn't noticed any Tall Oaks horses entered in that day's meet. Were they checking out Image?

With a squeal, Image kicked out with one leg, throwing Melanie onto her withers.

"Watch it!" Golden Idol's groom hollered.

Hot with embarrassment, Melanie regained her perch on the tiny saddle. Again Image had caught her not paying attention.

Jazz pulled off his sunglasses. "You all right?" he asked, searching her face. His voice was low, but she could hear his concern.

She forced a smile. "I'm just impatient to get going, like Image. And a little scared," she added in a whisper.

Reaching up, Jazz squeezed her hand. "Just remember the Florida Derby. You went into the race with everyone and everything against you. But you and Image did it—because you believe in each other. And I believe in *both* of you."

"Thanks." She squeezed his hand back. Then the outrider signaled the horses to head into the tunnel. Holding tightly to the lead, Jazz waited for Wave Dancer to enter, then followed the number four horse into the dark cave. At the end of the tunnel, the pony riders waited to escort them around the track.

Unhooking the lead, Jazz stepped away from Image. For a second Melanie's eyes locked on his. "Think Kentucky Derby," he whispered, then Image lunged forward into the bright sunlight. Melanie's stomach rolled. She wished Jazz hadn't mentioned the Derby.

A woman on a pinto fell into step beside them. When Image pinned her ears and lashed out with her teeth, Melanie thanked the woman but said she didn't need a pony horse. Still behind Wave Dancer, they jogged down the track, a wall of sound hitting them. The crowd was whistling and cheering. Image broke into a nervous jog, her back stiff and hunched beneath the saddle.

"You'd better chill, miss," Melanie warned as she posted awkwardly to the filly's jarring gait. Taking the reins in one hand, she laid her palm against Image's withers. "Relax. We've done this before. We can do this again." Melanie regulated her own breathing. *In and out.* Image bobbed her head and fought the bit. Then slowly, gradually, as they paraded clockwise in front of the grandstand, Melanie felt the filly's stride soften and her jaw yield to the pressure on the reins.

Yes! Melanie stroked the filly's neck, her frayed nerves calming somewhat. Image *was* listening. That was a good sign. Maybe they *could* win this race!

She squeezed Image into a warm-up canter. The starting gate was set up at the top of the homestretch. After the warm-up, the fillies headed for the gate. Flexing her fingers and sitting deep in the saddle, Melanie asked Image to walk. Shaking her head, the filly expressed her displeasure but eventually complied, breaking into a bouncy walk.

One by one the fillies loaded without mishap. Vicky Frontiere, mounted on Blushing Bride, caught Melanie's eye. She touched her whip to her helmet before her filly walked into the starting stall. Melanie smiled and gave her a quick thumbs-up. In front of her, Emilio Martinez, the so-called hotshot jockey, sat casually slouched on Wave Dancer as if he didn't have a care in the world. As soon as Dancer was loaded, the assistant starter headed for Image.

Suddenly Wave Dancer reared, then crashed forward into the padded front of the stall. Image startled and tried to wheel away from the gate. Melanie clamped a leg against her side. "She'll go in," she quickly told the starter. Using heels and hands, she got the filly aimed straight toward the stall. Still Image balked. She nervously flicked her ears, then, as if realizing she had no choice, scooted into the gate.

Melanie breathed a sigh of relief. In the number six

chute, Golden Idol struck the side, and the noise seemed to echo down the starting gate. *She's the one with the fast works*, Melanie remembered. That meant she'd probably set the pace. Melanie's strategy was to stay close behind Idol, then move up when the other filly burned out. Which was probably what Vicky, Steve, Tommy, and Martinez planned to do as well. A good start was essential. Image didn't like to hug the inside rail, but she also hated to run too wide or too far behind.

"One back!" The starter's call joggled Melanie from her thoughts. The last horse loaded quickly, and Melanie took a deep breath and laced the fingers of her left hand through Image's mane. The filly danced in the stall, her ears flicking.

The roar of the crowd filled Melanie's ears as she waited tensely for the bell.

3

WHEN THE BELL SOUNDED, IMAGE BROKE SO FAST THAT THEY were twenty strides down the track before Melanie's brain snapped into gear. *Rate her the first part of the race,* Jazz had said, which was sage advice in any race. Melanie glanced right and then left, trying to figure out their position in the field. Panic filled her when she suddenly realized she couldn't see any other horses.

Casting a quick look over her shoulder, Melanie caught sight of Glitter and Golden Idol, both several lengths behind Image. Behind them, the other fillies were strung across the track in the order in which they'd broken from the gate.

Melanie felt a sharp stab of fear as they blew past the grandstand and she began to tick off the seconds in her head. *Image was going too fast!* She, not Golden Idol, was setting the pace. Yet they still had about a mile to go! If Melanie didn't rein her in, the filly would burn out before they reached the finish line.

"Easy, girl. Save yourself," Melanie crooned, trying not to sound frantic, but her words were lost in the wind rushing past her cheeks. Sitting deeper, she tightened her hold on the reins. The filly's neck was arched, her stride so strong and powerful that the next distance pole flashed by before Melanie knew it.

That was when she realized that Image *was* rated! Melanie's heart flew into her throat. The filly was gliding down the track, her long legs effortlessly devouring the surface. Melanie tossed a look over her shoulder. They were at least four lengths ahead of the nearest horse. Elation rushed through her. At this rate, the other fillies couldn't touch her!

Wait, don't get too cocky. Visions of Image's first race filled Melanie's head. In that race, when the filly had gotten too far in front, she'd whirled to confront the oncoming field. Since then, Melanie had worked hard to keep her paced with the others. Only that hadn't worked in the Florida Derby. Image had had to wind her way around the other colts. Dirt had pummeled her face. The other horses had jostled her. And Image had hated it. Had the filly blown from the starting gate and taken the lead on purpose? Melanie laughed inwardly at the thought. And all this time, she'd been foolish enough to think *she* was calling the shots!

Switching leads, Image breezed around the backstretch turn. As they flew up the far side of the track, Image ran as smoothly as the motor of a Porsche. Still four lengths behind, the rest of the fillies galloped in a tight bunch, Glitter and Golden Idol in the lead. Melanie bit her lip. They were four furlongs from the finish line. Melanie could feel Image's energy still contained between her legs and hands; the filly's breathing was a rhythmic *hush, hush.*

They sailed around the homestretch turn with Melanie wondering, *Should I take a chance and just let her go?* Then she heard the thundering of hooves behind her. Steve Quinn on Incredible and Martinez on Wave Dancer had taken the lead from Golden Idol and Glitter. Both jockeys were pumping hard with their hands, making their moves. Side by side they battled, each trying to gain on Image.

Martinez raised his whip and Wave Dancer churned forward, steadily closing the gap. Image flicked one ear back as if assessing the situation. Afraid that Wave Dancer might catch them, Melanie chirped to her horse, but she didn't need to. Already she could feel the filly accelerate, as if changing gears, and in an instant Incredible and Wave Dancer fell behind.

Image had taken the lead, and she wasn't going to give it up.

The finish line rushed past before Melanie knew it. Image had led wire to wire, yet she was barely puffing.

Melanie pumped her fist in the air. Ever since she had first spotted the filly, she'd known in her heart that Image was special. Now they'd proven it to the crowd at Keeneland!

Melanie stood up in her stirrups, pulling hard, finally easing the filly into a canter. She ran one hand down Image's mane. "You did it!" she told the filly, breathless but elated.

They doubled back at a trot, and Jazz met them at the entrance to the winner's circle, hooking a lead to Image's bridle. Melanie leaped off the filly's back, and Jazz enveloped her in a hug. "Wow, what a race!" he cried as he swung her in the air. "It's on to the Kentucky Derby for *sure!*"

Flashbulbs popped, and reporters called out to Jazz: "Did you realize she won by six lengths?"

"Was taking the lead your strategy?"

"Did you think she'd lead wire to wire?"

Melanie was too excited to hear their questions. Pulling from Jazz's arms, she wrapped hers around Image's sweaty neck. "You were awesome!" Tears blurred her eyes. If she'd been alone, she would have broken down and sobbed with happiness and amazement. Image had blown away the day's competition, and Melanie had her answer.

Next stop, Kentucky Derby!

With a shake of her head, Image pranced sideways. Melanie swiped away her tears. Arching her neck, the filly stared across the racetrack as if posing for the photographers.

Jazz laughed. "Diva in action," he joked, giving Melanie a squeeze around her shoulders.

"Sir, we need your horse for the track photos," an attendant called to Jazz.

"Leg up?" Jazz asked Melanie. Putting one hand under her knee, he boosted her up. From her perch on Image's back, Melanie was able to see everything. At the backstretch turn, the other fillies were being led away by their grooms, and the jockeys were straggling tiredly toward the dressing room. In the stands, people cheered or booed when the payouts went up on the tote board. Incredible had come in second, Wave Dancer third. Clustered around Image, reporters and track officials scribbled on notepads and took photos. *It all seems unreal,* Melanie thought.

The track officials handed Jazz a trophy, and everyone posed for photos. Then Melanie dismounted, and a groom hurried over and took off Image's saddle. Melanie picked it up and headed for the scale.

"Weight's fine," the clerk of scales said when Melanie stepped on the scales. "Pretty win," he added in a matter-of-fact way, bringing a huge grin to Melanie's face.

Hopping off the scale, Melanie almost danced over to where Jazz held Image. Dirt and sweat crusted her cheeks, and her body felt as if she'd run ten miles, but she was too elated to care.

Jazz was speaking into a microphone held by an attractive brunette. Beside him, Image twirled in circles. As soon as Melanie walked over, the woman thrust a microphone in her face. Melanie couldn't help but notice her perfectly coiffed hair, cherry-red lipstick, and matching red nails. "Hello, Ms. Graham. I'm Janice Hart from WFHT. Are you elated by the win?"

"Definitely. I was worried when she ran such a fast first quarter, but then I realized she was running easily."

"Fast is right," Janice Hart declared. "The filly clocked at twenty-one and three-fifths for a quarter mile. Congratulations. So, Ms. Graham, you and your filly wear Whitebrook Farm colors. Yet I didn't see Ashleigh Griffen and Mike Reese here in the winner's circle. Aren't they celebrating this fabulous win with you?"

Melanie's jaw dropped. The reporter's tone had turned so snide that Melanie knew she was asking the question for only one reason: to get a reaction. The media loved conflict, especially if it sold newspapers or attracted viewers. "Of course they're proud of Image," she said quickly. "After all, Image is related to Wonder, Ashleigh's winning mare. But they're also busy, since they have several horses running today."

Ms. Hart smirked prettily. "Oh? I thought they might be upset since rumors have been flying that Perfect Image is bound for the Kentucky Derby. And we all know what *that* means—she'll be competing against Wonder's Star, their daughter's horse. Any comment?"

Melanie swallowed hard. She remembered Ashleigh commenting that if either Image or Star won, it would be great publicity for Whitebrook. Only now Melanie realized that wasn't true. Ashleigh, Mike, and Christina *were* upset that Image was racing against Star. That was why she'd been feeling such tension at Whitebrook. *But I'll never say that to you, Ms. Hart.*

Racking her tired brain, Melanie tried to come up with a neutral answer. But before she could reply, the reporter whipped around. Holding the microphone out toward Jazz, who still had Image's lead in his hand, Ms. Hart asked, "Comment, Mr. Taylor?"

"We're ecstatic with today's race results, of course," Jazz said smoothly, and Melanie noticed that the reporter not only was hanging on Jazz's every word but also clung to his arm as if afraid she might topple over on her spiked heels. "And yes, her strong performance in the Ashland Stakes clinches it—Image *will* be racing in the Kentucky Derby."

"Did you hear *that*, folks?" Janice Hart snapped around to face the camera. "Jazz Taylor, singer with the band Pegasus and owner of Perfect Image, winner of today's Ashland Stakes, has just announced that he's definitely running his filly in the Kentucky Derby! I bet we'll see some fireworks from Whitebrook Farm, home of Wonder's Star, as well as from the owners of *other* entries," she added dramatically. "Brad Townsend, to name one. So just remember you heard this breaking news from Janice Hart, WFHT News."

"Oh, I'll remember, all right," Melanie muttered. Snatching the reins from Jazz, Melanie hurried Image from the winner's circle. She'd had enough of the reporter's innuendoes about Ashleigh and Mike and every other owner of a Kentucky Derby entry—even if they were true.

4

JAZZ CAUGHT UP TO MELANIE AS SHE CROSSED THE RACE-track. "What's the rush?"

Melanie didn't slow down. "You could have talked to me before telling that reporter we were definitely running Image in the Derby."

"It's not like it's a big secret," Jazz countered as he fell into step beside her. "We've been talking about racing her in the Derby ever since she won in Florida."

"You just don't get it, do you?" Halting, Melanie pulled off her helmet. Her head felt hot enough to burst.

Jazz reared back as if she'd slapped him. "Obviously I *don't* get it. So why don't you explain to me what's going on?"

Melanie knew she wasn't being fair. But she also

couldn't talk about it now. "Look, I'm sorry. I didn't mean to snap at you," she apologized as she ran her fingers through her sweaty bangs. "And I'll explain later. But I've got to get to the jockeys' lounge or I'll be fined. And you've got to get Image to the test barn."

Handing Jazz the reins, she said good-bye to Image, then headed in the other direction. She knew Jazz was concerned, and she was rudely blowing him off. But he had a horse to cool down, and she needed to check in with the clerk in the jockeys' lounge. Besides, she needed time to put into words why she was so upset.

Two hours later Melanie was showered and on her way to Barn 32. She'd managed to avoid Christina by hiding out in the sauna. She didn't want to see her cousin until she'd had a chance to talk to Jazz about the dilemma that was pounding in her head. Fortunately, the Whitebrook horses had done well in all their races. Rascal and Fast Gun had come in second and Catwink third. If you counted Image, four Whitebrook horses had placed, which was a super accomplishment for any farm.

Only Melanie doubted that Ashleigh, Mike, and Christina were counting Image as a Whitebrook horse.

As she walked through the shed rows, grooms, trainers, and owners called out to her: "Super race!"

"Great ride!"

"Always knew that crazy filly would amount to something."

Melanie waved and smiled. As she rounded the side of a barn, a reporter from one of the Lexington newspapers caught up to her. "A second for an interview, Ms. Graham?" he asked, holding out his hand. "Brice Workman from the *Lexington Star*. I've been out to Whitebrook before."

Ignoring his hand, Melanie kept walking. She'd recognized the guy right away. He'd written many articles about Whitebrook horses, and she knew that he was knowledgeable and fair. But Melanie hated to deal with reporters. She always felt as though she ended up saying something stupid, so she usually let her dad, Jazz, or Ashleigh handle the media.

"Actually, what I'd love to do is write several articles on Perfect Image," Brice went on as he continued to walk beside her. Melanie glanced sideways at him. He was short and middle-aged with bowlegs and a limp. He looked like an ex-jockey, and Melanie wondered if the limp was a result of being tossed off one too many racehorses. "I'd like to follow you around for a week or two before the Derby," Brice said. "Report on Image's regimen, her training, that kind of stuff. Write it like a journal."

Melanie cocked her head. "I can't imagine all that would be interesting."

"You can't?" He stopped in his tracks, a puzzled

40

expression on his weather-beaten face. "A filly hasn't been a serious Derby contender since Winning Colors won in 1988."

Melanie frowned. Turning on her heel, she faced him. "Aren't you blowing this out of proportion, Mr. Workman? I mean, Image is a horse and the Derby is a horse race. It shouldn't matter if she's a filly or a colt."

For a minute Brice looked at her as if she really were crazy. Then he shook his head. "You really have no idea how huge this is going to be, do you?"

Melanie shrugged. "Well, sure. I mean, the Derby is always a big deal."

"You obviously *don't* have any idea," he said, still shaking his head. "And why should you? You're a kid."

Melanie bristled. "What do you mean by that?"

"Just what I said. Most of the trainers who have Derby entries have been at this business for decades." He slipped the tape recorder back into his jacket pocket. "They know that the media will do anything to snare audiences and attract advertisers. And horse racing is always trying to attract new fans. If Image does win, she'll be a filly ridden by a female jockey. The media love that kind of hook. They'll milk this for everything they can."

Melanie's brows rose. She'd never thought about that angle.

Pointing a finger at her, the journalist said, "If I were

you, I'd tighten your seat belt. For the next month, you and that rock singer are going to have one rough ride." Reaching into his other pocket, he pulled out a business card and handed it to her. "Take my word for it—the media will be all over you like sharks. So you'd better learn how to deal with them," he added before hobbling off. Melanie watched him until he disappeared.

The sun was setting, and a chilly breeze wafted around the corner of the nearest barn. She shivered. The reporter had left without pursuing the interview, yet he'd given her his business card. Weird.

She stuck the card into the back pocket of her jeans, then hurried to Barn 32. Joe had pulled the truck and trailer around front. The light was on in Image's stall, and she could see Jazz inside, brushing the filly.

Stopping, she leaned against the back of the trailer and watched them for a minute. Jazz was humming, his attention on Image, who quietly munched hay. Both were so dark and gorgeous it made her catch her breath. And both looked totally happy and peaceful. *Then why do I have such a feeling of dread in the pit of my stomach?* Melanie wondered.

"Melanie?"

Startled, Melanie jumped a foot. Joe was standing behind the trailer. "Joe! You scared me."

"Sorry. Who'd you think it was—some snoopy reporter?" he asked as he unlatched the doors.

"Why do you say that? Have there been reporters

around?" Stepping away from the trailer, she looked around nervously. Were Brice Workman's words coming true already?

"One or two. Ashleigh sent them off with a few terse comments."

"Oh." Melanie didn't even want to imagine what Ashleigh had said to them. She glanced over at Catwink's stall. A man and a woman she'd never seen before were standing outside. "Who're they?"

Turning away from her, Joe busied himself with the trailer doors. "Catwink's new owners."

Melanie sucked in her breath. "Catwink was claimed?" she whispered.

"'Fraid so. Trailer's ready for Image," he said, quickly changing the subject. "Only this time *I'm* driving," he added in such a firm way that Melanie didn't dare argue.

Not that she would have. She could barely breathe. She'd forgotten all about Catwink. Even though owners knew they were taking a chance when they entered a horse in a claiming race, they often had no choice. Should she tell Ashleigh she was sorry about Catwink, Melanie wondered, or would that only make things worse?

"Better get Image ready. We'll leave in half an hour," Joe said as he headed to the barn.

"Uh, right." Melanie wanted to sink back into the shadows. She looked over at Image's stall. Jazz was leaning on the top of the bottom door, looking at her. Image's head was silhouetted in the light behind him.

"The diva is walked, bathed, cooled down, and groomed," he said. "And if you're interested, I've also been walked, bathed, and cooled down. But I still need grooming." Jazz's black hair was straggling from his ponytail. And although he looked exhausted, he also looked cute enough to be posing for the cover of his next CD.

"And she looks gorgeous," Melanie told him. "Thank you. If you ever decide to quit singing for a million dollars a night, you can be Image's full-time groom. Unfortunately, the pay's not quite as terrific. Maybe six-fifty an hour?"

He chuckled.

Reaching out, Melanie smoothed a stray strand behind his ear, then wiped a smudge off his check. "Now *you're* groomed," she teased. Smiling apologetically, she added, "Sorry about my tantrum earlier. I guess Image's bad behavior is catching. And we do need to talk."

"Obviously." Jazz studied her face so intently that Melanie felt a flush rising up her neck. *Why can't I stay cool around the guy?* Dropping her gaze, she added, "But we can talk later. The trailer's ready. I'll get her shipping boots—"

"Melanie." Jazz put his hand on her arm. "You

don't need to rush off right this second. I want to hear about what's bothering you."

Just then Image gave a throaty nicker and shoved her head between Jazz and the door frame, pushing him out of the way. "Hey," he protested. "Is this the payment I get for giving you the greatest bath of your life?"

Melanie laughed and scratched under the filly's forelock. Image wiggled her lip. *If only things would stay this happy and simple*, Melanie thought. But she knew they wouldn't. Which meant she did need to talk to Jazz, and right away, before he headed back to his band and his tour.

"You're right, we do need to talk," Melanie began. "First, I was a little ticked by that TV reporter and her questions and comments. She's making us out to be some kind of party crasher. Like a filly shouldn't be invited to the Derby. Like we have no right to race against colts, and everyone's going to protest."

Jazz gave her a cool look. "Reporters love to stir up trouble. That's how they get ratings. We just need to be prepared for them."

Melanie shook her head. "I'm not sure we *can* be prepared." She told Jazz about her conversation with Brice Workman.

Jazz only snorted. "Melanie, I hate to brag, but the Derby is nothing compared to the attention the band

45

deals with every day. Believe me, we can handle the media."

"You mean *you* can. I always stick my foot in my mouth. And let's face it, Jazz, until your tour is over, you won't be around."

"I've got five more concerts," Jazz pointed out. "So I *will* be available for the last week before the Derby. I can't imagine things getting crazy any earlier than that."

Reluctantly Melanie agreed. She hated it when Jazz had an answer for everything. It made her sound like a whiny kid—just as the *Lexington Star* reporter had said. "Okay, I guess we can handle that part," Melanie conceded. "And who cares about the naysayers?" Reaching up, she stroked Image. "*We* know Image can handle the Derby. It's . . ." She hesitated, a lump rising in her throat.

"It's Ashleigh and Mike, right?" Jazz said softly.

Melanie's lower lip trembled. "And Christina and Cindy and Ben and Ian. If we race Image in the Derby, we're racing against my family, my *friends*. At first I thought it would be okay. But now I can feel them looking at me and Image like we're definite rivals."

"So that's what you meant earlier," Jazz said. "About things changing when you got back from Florida."

Melanie nodded. "And don't say I'm imagining it. Cindy and Ben were at the paddock before today's

46

race, and it wasn't to cheer me on. And I hated to hear Janice Hart say it, but she was right—Ashleigh and Mike *weren't* at the winner's circle today, because they *are* upset. Ashleigh and Christina have *huge* hopes for Star—Triple Crown hopes—and I think that mock race when Image almost beat Star scared the heck out of them.

"If we enter Image in the Derby, I'm afraid I'll lose them, Jazz," Melanie added miserably. "And I'm not sure one race is worth the risk."

5

A TEAR TRICKLED DOWN MELANIE'S CHEEK, HOVERED ON her chin, and plopped onto her arm. Using one finger, Jazz gently wiped the other tears away. "Now *I'm* sorry," he said. "I honestly didn't realize what was going on. Although I should have guessed."

Melanie shrugged. "There was no way you could have known. I just put it all together in my own head."

"Yeah, but I went through the same thing after my first album went platinum. I should have recognized what was going on with you."

"What do you mean?" Melanie asked him.

"Well, back home I had a lot of friends, most of them musical. All through high school we'd form bands, then break them up for one reason or another. Like, one time two of the guys didn't get along. One time the guitar player got a real job. Stuff like that. But we always stayed friends." Sighing, Jazz leaned on the top of the stall door and stared into the night. Melanie listened closely, one hand idly patting Image. "Things were cool when Pegasus first started," he went on. "You know, Nuke—I mean, Tommy—he's from my high school crowd. But the other members of Pegasus are guys I met who played in other bands. Guys who were serious musicians. When we first got together and jammed, I knew we had something special. We worked hard, practicing in my family's garage, and my friends would hang out and listen. But when 'Make My Day' hit the charts, things changed. Most of my friends couldn't handle it."

"What happened?"

"When I'd come back to visit, they'd pretend to be the same. But I could tell by their sarcastic jokes and remarks like 'Hey, Jazz, slumming today?' that they were jealous and angry at my success. Probably because they'd never gone anywhere with their own music."

"That must have been hard on you."

"It was very hard," he admitted. Turning sideways, he ran his hand down Image's neck. "These were guys I had grown up with. And suddenly they hated to be around me."

"Wow." Melanie ruffled Image's forelock. "But you obviously didn't let their jealousy stop you."

"I told myself, if they were really friends, they'd be proud of my success."

"And was it the right decision?"

He shrugged. "Well, to be honest, I lost a lot of friends. But I also found new ones." He smiled at Melanie, and she was stunned by the effect his smile had on her. Just like in that old cliché, she thought her heart would melt.

"Well," she said briskly. "The moral of that story is?"

Jazz chuckled. "You have to follow your dreams— no matter what."

"Even if it means hurting others?" Melanie glanced in the direction of Catwink's stall. Mike had joined Ashleigh and the other couple. Together the four were walking to the spare stall used as an office and supply room. She sighed. When Brice Workman had told her to tighten her seat belt, he'd been referring to hassles with the media. He didn't know that the real storm would be at Whitebrook. If Image ran in the Derby, could Melanie weather the next few weeks?

"Melanie, this is Image's *only* chance to race in the Kentucky Derby," Jazz said, cutting into her thoughts. "I think you have to ask yourself, 'How will I feel if I *don't* take this chance?'"

"You're right." Melanie dropped her hand. "The Florida Derby proved Image can handle a tough race against colts. Now I've got to show Image—and the world—I can handle the rest."

Jazz grinned. "Just remember, you're not doing it totally alone. Okay?"

"Okay. But you'd better finish that tour and get back here as soon as possible," Melanie said. "Seriously."

"Only because of the Derby?" he asked in a teasing voice. "Or will you miss me?"

Melanie blushed bright red. Before she could think of anything to say, Joe bustled up to the stall, hollering, "Are you guys getting Image ready to load?"

Melanie sprang away from the stall door. "We're almost ready, Joe. Honest," she said, sounding so flustered that Jazz burst out laughing, and Joe looked at them as if they were both out of their minds. Melanie laughed, too. *Remember this moment,* she told herself as she hurried to get Image's shipping boots. *It just might be the last time you laugh so heartily.*

"I can't believe it!" Christina pounded her hands on the Blazer's steering wheel. "There're reporters camped at the end of the driveway!"

Melanie glanced up from the open notebook on her lap. She'd been cramming for a chemistry quiz and hadn't been paying attention. It was the Thursday after the Ashland Stakes, and they were on their way to school. Christina had stopped at the end of the driveway. On the opposite side, several cars, and a van marked WFHT, were parked on the main road. Whipping out her cell phone, Christina began to punch in numbers. "I'm calling Dad. They've got to be doing something illegal."

Sighing, Melanie slid lower into the seat. Ever since the Ashland Stakes, Christina had been in a huff. And not without cause. The reporters had been relentless—phoning at all hours for interviews, catching the girls whenever they stepped off the property, asking them stupid questions: "Ms. Reese, are you and Ms. Graham still speaking?"

"Ms. Graham, when can we shoot photos of Image?"

"Ms. Reese, how is Star since his past illness? Able to handle a filly?"

"Ms. Graham, how do you feel about racing against your cousin?"

Per Jazz's advice on how to deal with the pesky media, Melanie had ignored them. But for some reason Christina wasn't able to tune them out, maybe because most of the questions revolved around the so-called rivalry between Image and Star or, worse, between Melanie and Christina.

"I'm so sick of them," Christina went on as she waited for someone to pick up on the other end of the phone. "Maybe if they asked intelligent questions about Star's training, or past races, or lineage. But all they can talk about—Hello? Ian? Can you tell Dad that there are hundreds of reporters down by the road?"

Melanie bit her lip to hold back a smile. *Hundreds?* Though if they didn't get moving, the few that *were* by the road would soon be beating on the windows. In fact, Melanie spotted a door opening and someone stepping from the van.

"Christina," Melanie whispered. "We've got to get—"

Angrily Christina waved at her to hush. "You mean there's nothing the police can do?" she asked indignantly. "Oh, all right."

Turning off the phone, Christina shifted the Blazer out of park and suddenly roared into the road, making a sharp left and narrowly missing a guy with a video camera. Melanie hung on to the door handle. Her notebook slid to the floor. "That was Ian's advice?" she joked. "Run over a few reporters?"

Christina glared at her. "This might be funny to you, but *I* don't see any humor here. I can't even drive to the mall without some reporter tailing me."

Melanie's smile faded. Picking up the notebook, she again tried to study. But the words and equations swam before her eyes in a blur. All week she'd tried to pretend that things were okay at home. Melanie had tried to talk to Christina, but her cousin had shrugged her off by saying that nothing was wrong and that

Melanie was just imagining things. Ashleigh spent a lot of time alone in the office, studying the Derby entries and plotting strategy. Whitebrook had never had a Triple Crown winner, and Melanie knew Ashleigh's hopes were on Star. And although Mike had been his usual self, everything he said sounded forced, as if he was trying too hard to keep things normal.

Even Ian, Kevin, and Samantha were acting strange. Melanie knew they were rooting for Cindy and Ben's horse, Gratis. In fact, everyone at Whitebrook was walking on eggshells, careful not to take sides or favor one horse over the other.

And it was only going to get worse, because they *all* wanted to win.

"The senior prom is coming up," Christina suddenly said, breaking the silence. "Can you believe it?"

Melanie glanced sideways at her cousin. With all the tension around the upcoming Derby, why was Christina bringing up something as silly as the prom?

"May twelfth. A week after the Derby."

Christina blew out her breath. Melanie studied her cousin for a second. Christina was dressed in tight flared jeans and a light blue T-shirt, her auburn hair blown out in a smooth, shiny waterfall down her back. She looked adorable, Melanie realized, while she'd just thrown on a pair of old jeans she'd found on the floor. It was as if Christina had gotten all dressed up for school. Melanie knew that all their friends were going to the prom. Was Christina lamenting the fact that she *wasn't* going?

"Why don't you ask Parker to take you?" Melanie suggested. "The Derby will be over by then, so you can relax a little."

"Parker?" Christina repeated with a look of shock.

"You *are* still friends," Melanie pointed out.

"Well, sure, but that would be like you going with Kevin."

"What would be wrong with that?" Melanie raised one brow. "Kevin and I would have fun. But that's not the point. I don't want to go to the prom," she countered. "Not even a teeny bit. And it sounds as if you do."

Christina frowned, her eyes on the road. "Not really. It's just that last night when I couldn't sleep, I started thinking that soon school will be over. Forever."

"Yes!" Melanie pumped her fist in the air. She couldn't leave Henry Clay fast enough.

Christina looked sharply at her. "Not everyone hates school as much as you do."

"Sorry." Melanie tried to look chastised, but failed. She'd been dreaming about being a full-time trainer and jockey for so long that two more months of school sounded like torture. "You just haven't mentioned anything about school or graduating in so long, I thought you were glad to get out, too."

"I *am*. It's just that with going to school part time, I

55

feel like we've missed so much. Football games, concerts, car washes, the spring dance, and now the prom." She sounded wistful. "Those are all experiences we'll never have again."

Thank goodness, Melanie wanted to say out loud, but she was so glad that she and Christina were talking again, she didn't dare. "Then I think you definitely should go to the prom," Melanie declared. "And don't tell me to forget Parker. I saw how jealous you were when he brought that girl to Whitebrook."

Christina laughed. "Until he told me she was his cousin."

"And he's *not* dating anyone," Melanie added.

"Are you sure? I know he's calling that girl he met in England."

"According to Kevin, he isn't. Not enough time, with university classes and getting two horses ready for the Olympics."

"Hmmm," Christina said thoughtfully as they turned into the school's parking lot. "I guess I could squeeze the prom between the Derby and the Preakness."

Melanie hoped that meant she was seriously thinking about the idea. Christina definitely needed something to cheer her up.

As soon as Melanie got to her first class, the teacher waved her over. "You're to report to Ms. Sheerer, your guidance counselor," he said, handing her a pass.

Melanie instantly panicked. What had she done now? Taking the pass, Melanie hurried from the classroom. Her heart was pounding. *This is worse than the start of a race.*

When she got to Ms. Sheerer's office, her palms were clammy. The young woman waved her inside and pointed to a chair. Melanie sat on the edge, her books balanced on her knees.

"You wanted to see me?" she asked.

Ms. Sheerer tapped the computer screen in front of her. "Yes. We need to talk about this semester's grades."

"Oh?" Melanie swallowed hard, preferring *not* to talk about them.

"We have two weeks left in this grading period and then one more grading period before graduation." Ms. Sheerer glanced over at Melanie. "You have passing grades in all your classes except chemistry. And unfortunately, you must have that science credit in order to graduate."

Melanie's mouth went dry. "Are you saying I may not graduate?"

"If you get an F either six weeks, you won't pass. That means summer school to graduate and you won't get a diploma on graduation day."

Then I quit. The three words popped into her head so fast that Melanie almost said them aloud. If she quit now, by summer she'd probably have won enough races to finally be a journeyman jockey. Staying in school had made it tough to get the forty-five wins, and she was tired of being a bug.

Then Melanie checked herself. For the last few years her father had supported her passion for horses and racing. All he'd asked was for her to maintain passing grades. If she quit school, he'd be so disappointed. Besides, there were only eight weeks left. She'd be foolish to quit now after hanging in there since ninth grade.

"So I just need two D's?" Melanie asked.

Ms. Sheerer nodded.

"I should be able to pull that off," she muttered to herself.

"We have tutoring available after school," Ms. Sheerer suggested. "And Ms. Black, your chemistry teacher, is always available."

Only I'm training a horse for the Kentucky Derby! Melanie wanted to shout. Maybe then Ms. Sheerer would understand why after-school tutoring wasn't high on her list of priorities.

Melanie stood up. "Thank you. I'll talk to Ms. Black." *And she'll ream me out,* she thought as she left the counselor's office. Before Melanie left for Florida, Ms. Black had given her makeup work to take with her. Melanie grimaced as she went down the empty hallway. Not that she hadn't tried to get the work done. Chemistry just made no sense. And since she couldn't think of one reason why she'd need chemical equations for a career in racing, she'd chucked the makeup work in the trash.

Stupid move, Graham. Melanie sighed. Part of her wished she were more like Christina, who made straight A's no matter how much time she spent riding. Part of her didn't care. If it weren't for her father, Melanie would have quit school ages ago.

But that's not the issue, she reminded herself. *Now you have to figure out a way to pass chemistry.*

Could she ask Christina for help? Melanie quickly shook her head. Christina was hardly talking to her. Kevin? He barely had time for his own classes since he was deep into spring soccer. Kevin's girlfriend, Lindsey? No to that, too, since she was also a soccer star. Then how about Katie?

That was it. Melanie decided to ask Katie Garrity, an old riding buddy, when classes changed. But when she caught up to Katie in the hall, her friend reminded her that she had the lead in the spring play and was really busy.

"Oh, the spring play. *Grease,* right?" Melanie asked.

Katie looked hurt. "No, that was last fall's production. This spring we're doing *Annie Get Your Gun.*"

"Oh, right." Melanie laughed, pretending as if she knew she'd been silly to forget such an important event. But inside she thought, *Boy, I am out of the high school loop.* "I'll try to make the show," she added,

59

though she knew she wouldn't. "You were great in *Grease*. Well, see you later. Gotta get to my next class."

As she headed to chemistry, Melanie racked her brains, trying to figure out who else could help her. Then it hit her. *Parker!*

He'd passed both Chemistry I and II. Although he was busy, his schedule was flexible. Melanie grinned, happy that she'd come up with such a great solution. Now she just had to explain to Ms. Black why she needed that makeup work *again*.

"So, Ms. Graham, I know there was some rivalry in Florida between Image and Speed.com," the reporter from the *Kentucky Times* said. "Now that Dustin Gates has definitely entered his colt in the Derby, are you anticipating any problems?"

"With the colt or with his trainer, Alexis Huffman?" Melanie quipped.

Everybody laughed. It was Thursday morning, a week later. Clustered in the grassy area between Whitebrook's barns, a dozen reporters waited to ask questions and take photos of Image and Star. Christina, Ashleigh, and Mike were also there with Melanie. All week long the reporters had been so pesky that Ashleigh had gotten an unlisted phone number for the farm. But that hadn't deterred them, and they'd started boldly driving up to the house. Hoping to appease their insatiable appetite for news about the two racehorses, Mike had finally invited the press to the farm. So far Melanie hadn't had any trouble dealing with their questions. But when the reporter brought up Speed.com, her stomach had instantly gone queasy.

Alexis Huffman had been a pain in Florida, causing trouble every chance she got. Melanie knew that Speed.com was Derby-bound, and she hadn't been looking forward to Alexis's arrival in Kentucky. However, since Alexis had left Lexington under suspicious circumstances, Melanie hoped the trainer would keep a low profile to avoid attracting the media's attention. "No, I don't expect any problems with Speed.com," Melanie said seriously. "Image beat him in the Florida Derby—fairly, I might add, even though Alexis protested the results. Speed.com's a great colt, but I believe that Image can beat him again."

Murmurs went through the group. "You sound pretty confident, Ms. Graham," another reporter called, his tone suggesting he didn't feel the same. "Especially for a novice jockey riding a *filly*."

Crossing her arms, Melanie glared at the man. It was about time that she let the world know that entering Image wasn't a gag or publicity stunt. "If I wasn't confident that Image could beat *all* the colts, I wouldn't have entered her in the Derby in the first place," she said firmly.

Beside her, Christina stifled a snort. Melanie

glanced sharply at her cousin. Christina's brows were raised, and she was looking at Melanie in disbelief. Even Mike and Ashleigh had skeptical expressions. Just then a barrage of flashbulbs went off.

Oh, great, Melanie thought. *By tomorrow it will be all over the newspapers.* She could see the words in her head: *"Trainer of Image brags, shocking the owners of Wonder's Star. Has this turned into a family feud?"*

"How about photos?" Mike said abruptly. "Ladies and gentlemen of the press, Image and Star are right this way, in the training barn."

As the reporters headed off, Melanie lagged behind. Part of her wanted to kick herself for her comment. Things were tense enough at Whitebrook. If she was smart, *she'd* keep a low profile, too. At the same time, Melanie was sick of all the naysayers. All week the news had been full of analysts saying that there was no way Image, an unproven filly, could win against the colts entered in the Derby. They'd rattled off facts and statistics. They stated that Image's second-place finish in the Florida Derby was a fluke. They acted as though they knew what they were talking about. *Only none of them knows Image,* Melanie told herself. *So how can they say she can't possibly win?*

As she headed to the barn to join the others, Melanie thought for the hundredth time how she wished Jazz were there. Christina had Ashleigh and Mike for support. Melanie felt very alone.

Not that she wasn't getting plenty of support from the public. Image had gotten hundreds of fan letters—mostly from girls excited to see a filly in the Derby who was also ridden by a girl. *Which might be part of Christina's problem*, Melanie realized. Star the wonder colt was suddenly not the star anymore.

As Melanie rounded the corner into the barn, Christina stepped into her path. "*All* the colts?" Christina quipped, repeating Melanie's words. "That means you expect to beat Star, don't you?" Hands on her hips, she glared at Melanie, her eyes flashing.

Melanie caught herself. *Careful. Watch what you say.* But then she realized she was tired of tiptoeing around everybody at Whitebrook, hiding how she really felt. "Yes. I do expect Image to beat Star," Melanie said. Crossing her arms, she met Christina's gaze.

Christina's eyes narrowed. "I don't believe you. I think you know there's *no way* Image can win. I think you and Jazz are doing this for some publicity stunt. And why not? Jazz is used to the limelight. And you certainly *love* to be the center of attention."

Melanie took a step back, startled by Christina's harshness.

"Otherwise, why else would you do it?" Christina continued, her angry words mixed with tears. "You *know* how much it means to us to have Star win. It's the most important thing in the world to my mom—and to *me*. Telling everybody that Image can beat Star? Racing her against us? It's bad enough we lost Catwink because of you and Image. Now this! Is this how you repay us for all we've done for you?" she added. Whirling, she hurried to join the reporters in the aisle, leaving Melanie alone and stinging.

6

"FIGURE OUT THE EQUATION FOR THAT CHEMICAL REAC-tion," Parker said that evening, "and write it in here." He pointed to a blank space on the worksheet. Barely hearing him, Melanie sat hunched over the kitchen table, staring gloomily at her open chemistry book. Try as she might, she couldn't concentrate on the makeup sheet in front of her. Christina's words still rang in her head, making it ache. *Is she that angry?* Melanie asked herself over and over. *So angry that we'll never be friends again?* Melanie had been so hurt, she hadn't dared to talk to her cousin since. Not that Christina's behavior invited discussion. Even though her cousin seemed to have calmed down, she'd avoided Melanie all day.

"Melanie? If you want my help, I'll stay," Parker

said, glancing at his watch. "But I've got a mess of stuff to do tonight."

Melanie bolted upright in the chair. "Oh, sorry! Please, stay. I really need help. I've got a chemistry quiz tomorrow. And all this makeup work's due. The Derby's in nine days, and it's so hard to concentrate...."

Just then Christina came into the kitchen, and Melanie let her words trail off.

"Oh, hi, Parker!" Christina greeted him cheerfully as she opened the refrigerator door. "I didn't know you were here."

Right, Melanie thought, noting how cute Christina looked in short shorts and a tiny knit top—hardly her usual after-dinner outfit.

"Hey, Chris." Parker gave Christina a huge smile. "I'm helping Melanie with chemistry."

Pulling an apple from the refrigerator, Christina shut the door and leaned back against it. "Cool," she said as she took a bite. Melanie glanced from Parker to Christina and back again. The two were just staring at each other with goofy smiles.

Abruptly Melanie stood and pushed back her chair. "Hey, do I ever need a bathroom break," she said. "Be right back, Parker. Don't go away. We're almost done with this sheet."

Parker nodded, but his attention was still on Christina. "So what have you been up to lately?" he asked her. "Besides getting Star ready for the Derby."

"Oh, don't mention that word," Melanie said under her breath as she left the kitchen. "I don't need Chris to go ballistic again."

As Melanie passed the door to Ashleigh's office, she peered inside. Her aunt was sitting at her desk, leafing through a book. Melanie looked closer. It was a photo album. Melanie scuttled past, hoping her aunt hadn't seen her. As the Derby grew closer, Ashleigh grew more nostalgic, often mentioning Pride, Champion, and other Whitebrook horses who had raced in the Derby . . . and reminding Melanie of Christina's accusations, especially about how Catwink was gone and it was her fault.

Sighing, Melanie went into the small bathroom, shut the door, and locked it. *Maybe I'll just stay in here forever.*

A few minutes later someone knocked on the bathroom door. "Melanie?" It was her aunt's voice. "Telephone. It's Jazz."

"Thanks, I'll take it upstairs." Hurrying, Melanie finished washing her hands. As she took the stairs by twos, her heart started beating with excitement.

"I'm so glad you called!" Melanie blurted when she picked up the phone on her bedside table.

"You won't be glad when I give you the news," Jazz said, his voice sounding distant and tired.

Melanie's heart sank.

"I'll still be there next week, before the Derby," he

continued. "But not as soon as I thought. Your dad arranged for the band to play Tuesday morning on *Live with Reginald and Katie.* Monday we have to fly to New York City."

"What a great opportunity," Melanie said, trying to sound enthusiastic.

"I'll head to Lexington right after that—I've already got the plane ticket. I'll be there Tuesday night."

"Super. And don't worry about Image. She's incredible. I've been trying to keep her fit and interested by varying her morning workouts—kind of like I did in Florida."

There was a pause, then Jazz said, "Actually, it wasn't Image I was worried about. I know you're taking the best care of her. But how are *you* doing? I've been reading the Kentucky papers. They're really playing up the rivalry between Image and Star."

Melanie sighed as she slumped on her bed. "And Image and Speed.com, and Image and Gratis. The only one who isn't getting much press is Brad and Celtic Mist. And I bet he's not happy about that."

"That didn't answer my question."

"Right." Melanie twirled a few strands of hair around her finger. "Um, I'm doing okay. Image and I are getting lots of fan mail. I've saved some of the best. Girls write stuff like 'Girl jockeys rule—and so do their fillies.' This morning Mike invited the press to the farm. I'm hoping the reporters got their fill of Star and Image for a few days."

Jazz snorted. "I doubt that. Uh, how are things between you and Chris?"

"She's barely speaking to me," Melanie replied honestly. She didn't want to tell Jazz about her cousin's outburst. "Not that I blame her," she added quickly. "She wants to win this Derby more than anything. I mean, before she was saying things like 'Oh, we can work together to get both our horses ready for the Derby.' But I think now she realizes I'm dead serious about winning."

"I'm sorry I can't be there to help," Jazz said. "But the good news is that Susan and your dad are flying with me from New York. We'll all be there to cheer you on."

A smile broke out on Melanie's face. "That will be wonderful." They talked for a few more minutes. When they both hung up, Melanie felt renewed, ready to handle anything. Even chemistry.

She was about to leave the bedroom when her gaze landed on the bronze statue of the Thoroughbred that Christina had given to her to mend the rift between them when Raven had been injured. Melanie thought back to how furious she'd been at her cousin when Raven broke down during the race. Now Christina was furious with her. Were things ever going to get better between them? As she approached the kitchen, she could hear Parker and Christina talking. Were they discussing the prom? Had Christina asked Parker to go with her?

But then she heard Christina say "Image" and "I'm angry at her," and Melanie stopped in the hallway.

"Look, Chris," Parker's deeper voice said, "you're going to have to get over it. Melanie has every right to run against you in the Derby. In fact, she'd be stupid not to. It would be like me telling Lyssa Hynde she couldn't compete against me in an event just because I didn't want her to."

Thank you, Parker.

Christina sniffed. "True. But admit it, Parker, you've been plenty mad at Lyssa and her horse."

Parker chuckled.

"I know in my head that Melanie and Image deserve to be in the Derby just as much as Star and me," Christina continued. "And maybe if the media weren't making such a big deal, I wouldn't be so upset. It's just that . . ."

Melanie strained to hear the rest, but her cousin's words grew too faint. Then she heard the scrape of a chair, as if someone was getting up, and popping sounds, and she knew she'd better quit eavesdropping.

"Sorry I took so long," she said loudly as she strode into the kitchen. Parker and Christina were standing close together in front of the microwave, watching a bag of popcorn. The two sprang apart as if they'd been doing something they shouldn't. "That was Jazz on the phone," Melanie explained as she took her seat at the table.

"How is he?" Parker asked.

"Great. He'll be here next week. Maybe we can all do something together." She glanced from Christina to Parker. Turning, Christina opened the microwave and pulled the hot bag from the microwave.

"Sounds like a good idea," Parker said. "Chris?"

Looking over her shoulder, Christina smiled hesitantly. "Sure. Why not?" she replied, but her eyes wouldn't meet Melanie's. "Maybe a movie. Or bowling. Something fun that has *nothing* to do with the Kentucky Derby."

Melanie grinned. "We won't mention horses once."

Parker chuckled as he sat beside Melanie. "Like that will ever happen."

Christina brought over the bowl of popcorn, and they all dug in. As Parker started in again on chemistry, Melanie let out a relieved breath. A truce—at least for the night.

Saturday morning Melanie finished cooling Image, turned her out into her paddock, and then headed back to the training barn. Ashleigh and Mike were starting a slew of two-year-olds. That meant spending a lot of time grooming, bridling, saddling, leading, mounting, and dismounting. The young colts' and fillies' bones were too soft for hard work, but there was still plenty to do. Melanie was grateful for the work. It kept her—and everyone else—too busy to talk about the Derby.

Only a week to go, she thought as she walked across the dewy grass. When Melanie entered the training barn, Ashleigh stood in the aisle with a clipboard and pen. Christina and Dani were already there, helmets in their hands, both sweaty and dusty from morning works. So were Ian, Joe, and Kevin. "Christina, you have Radar and Domino. Stalls seven and eight," Ashleigh was instructing. "After you groom and tack them up, Ian will help you belly them." She pointed her pen at Ian. "I don't need to remind you to watch Domino. He's been giving Dani a hard time. Dani, you have Susannah and Jewel. Joe will work with you. Melanie, you're assigned Frog and Lily. Kevin will help you."

Melanie rolled her eyes. *Frog!* She'd worked with the bratty colt before. He kicked, bit, and reared.

Beside her, Kevin chuckled. "So the princess got the frog," he teased. "Maybe if you kiss him, he'll turn into a prince."

"Except I'm no princess. Maybe *you* should kiss him," Melanie joked right back as she headed into the tack room. Grabbing a grooming bucket, she followed the others from the tack room. Ashleigh was still in the aisle, talking to Jonnie, one of the stable hands.

When the group passed the barn office, Mike suddenly threw open the door. "The phone's ringing off the hook, and it's not even nine o'clock," he announced. "Somehow the press got our unlisted number."

Everybody groaned. "Now what do they want?" Ian asked. "They've already asked every possible question."

"Not *every*." Mike's gaze zeroed in on Melanie, and her stomach jumped. "Seems Dustin Gates, Speed. com's owner, has been shooting off his mouth about the race in Florida, and the reporters want to know if he's telling the truth about Image or not. They want a comment from you, Melanie. *Now*, or they'll print whatever they want."

All heads turned toward Melanie. She smiled weakly. "Well, uh, I have no idea what Mr. Gates is saying about Image, so I can't comment."

Ashleigh frowned. "That's not the point, Melanie," she said, hugging the clipboard to her chest. "The point is that any minute another barrage of reporters will be attacking the farm. We haven't had a normal day since Janice Hart announced you were definitely running Image in the Derby."

Melanie's face paled. Were they totally blaming her for all the reporters' high jinks?

"We just don't have the security and personnel to handle all this unwanted attention." Ashleigh waved her arm around, indicating the farm. "We could handle it if it were just Star racing in the Derby. But since Image is a filly, and you're a girl, the media has blown the race *way* out of proportion. We've had reporters calling from almost every state. Yesterday a guy with New York license plates drove up. Said he wanted to write a book about you and Image! It's like a *circus* around here."

Melanie's mouth went dry. "What are you saying?"

"I'm not sure what I'm saying," Ashleigh blurted. Turning abruptly, she strode from the barn. There was a moment of silence as everyone watched her go. Then Mike went back into the office, closing the door firmly behind him, and the rest of the crew slowly filed out of the barn.

Melanie stood rooted to the spot. She'd been living at Whitebrook for almost five years. But now, for the first time, she felt like an intruder.

That night Melanie skipped dinner, excusing herself by saying she wanted to finish the last of her chemistry makeup work. Which was true—it just wasn't the whole truth. There was no way she could sit at the dinner table in awkward silence with Ashleigh, Mike, and Christina.

As she worked on her equations, she glanced at

the phone. She wished she could talk to Jazz. That morning Ashleigh had seemed to run out of patience with the situation. Melanie had no idea what to do. She couldn't deal with the media by herself. But Mike and Ashleigh were making it clear that they were fed up.

Although the phone had been ringing all night, Melanie knew it wasn't Jazz calling. Right now he was onstage, singing and playing the guitar. Closing her eyes, she tried to visualize him performing. He had a great voice and a super stage presence. Just the thought of him brought a smile to her face. A knock on the bedroom door made her smile freeze.

"Mel?" Christina opened the door and peered inside. "Parker and I are going to Louisville for fireworks. Part of the Derby Festival. Want to come?"

Melanie shook her head. "Thanks for asking, but I need to finish this up before Monday." She held up the paper she was working on.

"Oh, too bad," Christina said, but Melanie thought her cousin looked relieved. *She doesn't want to be with me, either*, Melanie thought gloomily.

"And I mean that," Christina added quickly. "I wish you could come with us. Only . . ."

Melanie held her breath. Was Christina finally going to admit how mad she was? Maybe if they got it out in the open, things between them wouldn't be so strained.

"Only I kind of want to spend some time alone with Parker," Christina continued, her cheeks turning pink. "I've decided to take your advice and ask him to the prom."

"Oh!" Melanie blurted, surprised at Christina's words. "I mean, that's awesome."

"Yeah," Christina said with a dreamy smile. "Well, have fun with chemistry."

"Sure."

Christina shut the door, and Melanie sighed. Maybe asking her to go to the fireworks had been Christina's way of patching things up. Minutes later, she heard Christina holler good-bye to her parents, then the front door slammed, Parker's truck rumbled up the drive, and the house was quiet.

Melanie slumped back on her pillow. It was a week before the greatest race of her life, and all she felt was depressed. Her bedside phone rang again. Melanie didn't even glance at it. Mike had gotten caller ID so he could screen the calls. When it continued to ring, Melanie knew it must be another radio, newspaper, magazine, or TV reporter. Ashleigh was right. They *were* relentless.

She plugged her ears, trying to drown out the sound. A half hour and ten phone calls later, she finally sprang from the bed, her chemistry work in hand. Maybe it would be quieter on the front porch.

Melanie settled into the porch swing. The sun had set, and the night air was cool. Spring peepers chirped in the oak trees, and she heard a horse whinny. Reluctantly Melanie picked up her last worksheet. She studied for about thirty minutes, but the porch light was dim, and it was hard to read the words. Fortunately, Parker had helped her make sense of the equations, but it was still tough to get excited about the periodic table.

In the distance, Melanie heard the *thump-thud* of a horse's hooves. She could tell it was coming from Image's paddock. Holding her breath, she listened. The sound wasn't rhythmic, as if Image were trotting across the pasture to join Baby. It was irregular, as if Image was shying at something.

A loud snort made her sit up.

Was something spooking the filly?

Jumping from the swing, Melanie leaped down the porch steps and jogged across the grass, toward Image's paddock. There was no moon, the sky was dark, and she had trouble seeing. When she reached the fence, she scanned the paddock. Baby was by the gate staring mournfully into the empty feed bucket. There was no sign of Image.

Then a flash of light illuminated the filly, who was standing stiffly in the far corner. *What in the world is going on?* Melanie climbed over the fence and headed toward Image. Was someone in there with her? Was Joe or Dani checking on the horses? "Hey!" she called, hoping to hear a familiar "hey" back.

A tall shadow took off, running away from Melanie. Stunned, Melanie halted to catch a better look. It was a person, dressed all in black. A cry rose in her throat. Someone was trying to hurt Image!

MELANIE TOOK OFF RUNNING. "HEY, YOU, STOP!" SHE screamed, furious that someone would dare to mess with her horse. She'd gone through the same scare in Florida. Worried that someone—Alexis—might try to harm Image, Melanie had even slept in the filly's paddock.

Vaulting the fence, the dark shadow raced across the mare and foal pasture, in the direction of the main road. Melanie reached the far fence in time to see the figure disappear over a hill. If the person had a car waiting, there was no way that Melanie was going to catch up.

Heart thumping, she spun around to make sure Image was all right, almost bumping into the filly, who was tagging along behind her. "Image!" Melanie ran her hands over the horse's sides and legs.

Behind them, a light bobbed and someone called, "Melanie? What's going on? We heard you yelling."

Melanie recognized Mike's voice. "I'm over here, Uncle Mike. Checking on Image. Someone was in the paddock with her." Tugging on Image's mane, Melanie steered the filly toward the gate.

Mike met her there, flashlight in hand. Beyond him, Ashleigh stood on the porch, her arms crossed. "Is everything all right?" her aunt called.

"Everything's okay!" Mike hollered back. Then he aimed the light at Melanie. "*Is* everything all right?"

Tears of anger sprang into her eyes. "I think so, except someone was in the paddock with Image. Some stranger. The person took off across the pasture, toward the road. It was so dark I couldn't even tell if it was a man or a woman. And I had no idea what he or she was doing."

Mike turned and aimed the light down White-brook's long driveway. In the distance, a car motor roared as if someone was driving away. "Sounds like it's too late to find out who it was and what they were up to," he said wearily.

Melanie walked around Image. The filly looked fine. Then she gazed into her eyes and checked her nostrils and mouth. There were no weird smells or substances.

"What are you looking for?" Mike asked.

Melanie shook her head. "I don't know. I guess I'm

paranoid that someone might try to hurt Image before the Derby."

Mike frowned. "I doubt that. Those days of doping the competition's horse are over. Still, this is serious. We can't have strangers trespassing day and night."

"When I first ran out, I saw a flash of light," Melanie told him. "Maybe it was some snoopy reporter taking a photo. Although why they wouldn't call and ask for permission is beyond me."

"I can tell you why—we've stopped answering their calls," Mike explained. "There are too many to respond to anymore—most from out of state. Some from overseas. Obviously, the press conference didn't solve the problem." He ran his fingers through his hair in a frustrated gesture. "Melanie, I know these past weeks have been as hard on you as they have been on us. But it's only going to get worse. And well, Ashleigh's outburst wasn't very tactful this morning, but she's right—Whitebrook isn't equipped to handle this kind of attention."

"I'm so sorry, Uncle Mike," Melanie murmured. "I realize now how naive I was. I had *no* clue that riding a filly in the Kentucky Derby would be such a big deal."

"Actually, I didn't, either," Mike admitted. "The media's really playing it up as a girl-versus-guys thing. It's definitely not just a horse race anymore, which must be why it's attracting so much crazy attention. Tomorrow Ashleigh, Ian, and I will discuss the problem. We may have to hire security guards." He waved his arm around the farm. "But no matter what we do, it's hard to secure a hundred acres of pasture and woods. Which means Image may not ever be safe."

Melanie grimaced. She wasn't quite sure what Mike was trying to say. But she knew something needed to be done to keep her horse and Whitebrook safe. "This isn't your problem," she finally said. "It's mine. Let me talk to Jazz and figure out what to do."

"All right, but we need to be in on the decision, too. You *are* family, Melanie." He patted her shoulder. "And don't forget it."

Turning, he strode off. Ashleigh had already gone inside. Sighing deeply, Melanie stroked Image's black nose, her hand trailing off at the snippet of white. "What are we going to do?" she asked the filly.

Baby ambled over. "You're some watchdog," Melanie told the fuzzy pony sarcastically as she scratched under her forelock. "Looks like tonight, at least, I'm camping under the stars." Sighing again, she patted Image and headed back into the house.

The door to Ashleigh's office was closed, and she could hear her aunt's and uncle's voices. Melanie didn't have to wonder what they were talking about. And she knew they were right—something had to be done. It wasn't just the security she was worried about. It was the mounting tensions between her and the family. Derby day was nearing, and it was only going to get worse. *Okay, so you know what the problem is. Now what's the solution?* As Melanie trudged upstairs to get a sleeping bag and pillow, she realized she had no idea.

Hours later, Melanie whacked her pillows, still trying to get comfortable. She'd put down a tarp, sleeping bag, quilt, and two pillows. She'd brought out a stuffed teddy bear, a book, a flashlight, and a bowl of popcorn. But the ground was hard, she couldn't read by flashlight, and the teddy bear wasn't much company.

For a little while, Image and Baby hung around on the other side of the fence. But they'd soon gotten bored and wandered off to graze. It was almost midnight, and Melanie was still too wired to sleep, still too full of questions with no answers. What was she going to do with Image?

Car lights came into view, and Melanie heard the sound of Parker's truck. Propping herself up on one arm, she watched the truck stop in front of the house. Minutes later she saw Christina and Parker go inside.

Hands clasped behind her head, Melanie sank back on the pillows. Had Christina gotten up the nerve to ask Parker to the prom? If she had, that meant buying a new dress and matching shoes, getting her hair done—all those frilly, fun things that Melanie hadn't thought about since she'd started seriously racing. This was her last year at Henry Clay. Would she regret not going to the prom?

She certainly hadn't participated in many school activities. She'd watched a couple of Kevin's baseball games and soccer matches. She'd seen Katie in one play. She'd . . . Melanie thought hard, trying to remember if there was anything else. At one time she'd been interested in art, like her mom. But since she'd been at Henry Clay, she hadn't even taken one drawing class. Her sole focus had been horses, especially since she'd gotten Image.

Which is why I'm camped out with two horses instead of on a hot date.

Suddenly a black shadow loomed over her. "Melanie?"

She sat up with a scream.

"It's just me." Parker stooped next to the sleeping bag.

Melanie put her hand over her heart. "You scared me half to death!"

"Sorry. Ashleigh and Mike told us what happened. Are you on guard duty?"

"Yeah. I'm not sure what else to do." Melanie gazed in the direction of the pasture. "If Image could be kept in a stall all night, we could at least watch her over the video monitors. But you know how she is—she'd freak."

"Mmm. That is a problem." He glanced back at the house. "According to Christina, that's not the *only* problem."

Melanie groaned. "I bet she gave you an earful."

"Sort of." Parker was silent for a minute. "You know, I might have a solution."

"Really?" Drawing up her knees, Melanie clasped her arms around them and leaned forward, eager for *any* suggestions.

"Let me think on it for a night and talk to you tomorrow."

"You can't tell me now?"

He shook his head, then gave her a secretive smile. "Not yet."

"Oh, all right." Melanie gave him an exaggerated pout. "But first thing tomorrow." She waved her arm, indicating her setup. "I don't think I can handle another night of these plush accommodations!"

Sunday morning, Melanie was trotting Image in the back pasture. An unusual routine for a Derby entry, she knew. But long ago she'd learned that the filly needed daily exercise, and constant works around a track were too hard on her three-year-old legs. Plus it got boring, and Image found ways to get into trouble. Melanie discovered that even in Florida, a long ride on trails or around fields helped keep the filly mentally and physically fit. *All great reasons to be out here,* Melanie thought as they trotted up the hill toward the woods. *But let's face it, Graham, you're also trying to avoid Christina and Star.*

The duo had headed out to the track right before Melanie and Image. Melanie hadn't talked to her cousin since her date the night before with Parker. On weekdays they bumped into each other as they were getting ready for morning works. But Sundays were usually a day off, so Christina had slept late. She wasn't awake when Melanie straggled into the house dragging her sleeping bag, quilt, and pillows. And by the time she'd showered and gone downstairs, Christina was at the barn.

A rabbit popped from a patch of high grass and zigzagged across the pasture. Snorting in mock terror, Image ducked her head and hunched her back. Melanie dug her heels in the filly's side and drove her forward. "No bucking," she warned. "I'm already stiff and sore from sleeping on the ground all night!"

And sleepy, she added with a yawn. Not a good combination for preparing to ride in the biggest race of her life.

Which brought her back to Parker and his possible solution. What did he have in mind?

"Okay, girl, a slow breeze along the fence," Melanie said as she squeezed Image into a canter. It was the perfect place. The fence line wound up a slight incline, working Image's hind muscles. And Melanie had ridden along it enough times to know there were no dangerous holes and the ground wasn't punishingly hard. As soon as she felt Melanie's legs against her side, Image playfully tossed her head and leaped forward. They cantered up the hill, Image's ears pricked, her attitude joyful. The filly's long stride was so powerful and effortless that Melanie broke into a huge smile. *This is why we're entered in the Derby*, Melanie thought. *This is why we've got a good shot at winning. Because Image loves to run.*

"Melanie!"

The sound of someone calling her name interrupted her reverie. Melanie glanced down the hill. Parker stood at the bottom by the gate. He was waving his arm, trying to get her attention.

Sitting deeper in the saddle, Melanie asked Image for a quiet transition down to a trot. But the filly was having too much fun. Rooting her head, she jerked the reins through Melanie's sweat-slicked fingers and took off at a dead run. "Image!" Melanie growled angrily. Quickly she regained her balance and shortened her hold on the reins. Image was just being foolish, but Melanie couldn't afford to have her strain a muscle or pull a tendon. Tightening the right rein, she forced the filly closer to the fence. When they reached the corner, Melanie sat deep and used a pulley rein to turn Image hard into a circle. The filly protested with a halfhearted buck, then skidded to a rough halt.

Melanie blew out a relieved breath. "You are so bad," she scolded. "What if we'd plowed into the fence? Or you'd tripped and fallen? Now come on— let's see what Parker wants. If we're lucky, he has the answer to our problems."

Melanie walked Image the long way down the grassy hill, letting her cool off. When they reached the bottom, Parker was no longer by the gate. Melanie hoped he wasn't with Christina. She didn't want to discuss anything about Image in front of her cousin.

She was dismounting when a man's deep voice said, "Here, let me open the gate for you."

Melanie dropped to the ground. She'd know that voice anywhere. It was Brad Townsend, Parker's father.

Taking her time, Melanie patted the filly's neck, pulled the reins over her head, and only then peered around Image's head and said with exaggerated politeness, "Why, hello, Mr. Townsend. What brings you to Whitebrook so early on a Sunday?"

Nothing good, that's for sure. In all the years Melanie had lived at Whitebrook, Brad Townsend, owner of Townsend Acres, the biggest Thoroughbred farm in Lexington, had brought nothing but trouble. Competitive to a fault, Brad didn't hesitate to use his wealth and influence to get what he wanted. *Except for Image and Star,* Melanie thought gleefully. Two of Lexington's fastest three-year-olds had eluded him. As revenge, he'd spent several million dollars to purchase Celtic Mist, a stakes-winning colt from California, who was also entered in the Derby.

"*Image* brings me to Whitebrook," Brad said as he eyed the filly. As always, Brad looked the part of the country gentleman in a tweed sport coat, pressed tan slacks, and polished tasseled loafers.

Melanie bristled. "Haven't you given up on adding Image to your collection of trophies?"

Brad chuckled. "Always feisty, aren't you, Melanie? You still haven't learned how to be a gracious southern belle."

Melanie rolled her eyes. Turning, she loosened Image's girth. The filly stuck out her nose, slobbering on Brad's coat sleeve. Without a word, he pulled a handkerchief from his pocket and wiped it off.

"Actually, I have no interest in *purchasing* Image. My only interest is beating her in the Derby. Which, I might add, Celtic Mist will accomplish effortlessly, although the filly did look fantastic racing *wildly* across the field." He chuckled, and Melanie knew he wasn't trying to be complimentary.

Don't lower yourself by responding, Melanie told herself as she walked around Image to raise the stirrup on the far side. Leaning on the top rail, Brad continued to eye Image with an appraising look.

"Then what *is* your interest in Image?" Melanie finally asked.

"Parker mentioned that Whitebrook was having security problems."

Melanie froze, her hand on the stirrup leather.

"As you know, Townsend Acres has an excellent security system. Not only do I have guards who regularly patrol the farm, but every area—outside and inside—is monitored with security cameras."

Turning slowly, Melanie stared at him. Had Brad come here to brag about his farm? "Your point?"

Brad smiled graciously. "I'm inviting you and Image to stay at Townsend Acres until the Derby is over."

8

MELANIE BLINKED. IMAGE STAYING AT TOWNSEND ACRES? *This* was Parker's solution? "Are you serious?"

Brad arched one brow. "I don't joke about anything that has to do with Thoroughbreds, Melanie. And why wouldn't I be serious?"

"For one thing, Image will be competing against your horse. Isn't that a conflict of interest or something?"

Brad laughed. "She may be in the same race as Celtic Mist, but I don't consider her competition. And neither do the media clowns," he added derisively. "A filly in the Derby? A winning lady jockey? Those are entertainment ploys that everyone hopes will increase ratings or interest in horse racing."

So he doesn't think we have a chance. Melanie snapped

the stirrup leather, and Image danced sideways. *Boy, will he be shocked.*

"Especially since I've hired Emilio Casados to ride," he added as if it were an afterthought. Melanie wasn't surprised by his choice. Casados had ridden the previous year's Derby winner, plus he was Jockey of the Year. Brad *would* buy the best for Celtic Mist.

"Good choice," Melanie said blandly. Throwing open the gate, she led the filly through, steering her dangerously close to Brad, hoping Image would stomp all over his fancy tasseled shoes.

Putting one hand on the filly's flank, Brad pushed her away, then fell into step beside Melanie. "Actually, bringing Image to Townsend Acres was Parker's suggestion," he explained. "But I agreed that it was a good solution when he told me how relentless the media have been. I don't wish to see Image hurt, nor do I wish to see you or Star drop out of the Derby. The increased publicity about your rivalry has been terrific for horse racing in general."

Melanie halted. "Parker said we were going to drop out?"

"Not at all. He merely stated that the stress was getting to everyone here. And that's not a criticism of you, the Reeses, or Whitebrook," he added quickly. "It's a statement of the times—everyone wants to make a buck off the Derby. That means people will do anything to get their story. It's the reason I strengthened Townsend Acres' security several years ago. I can offer your filly a private paddock and premier training facilities, and you a guest apartment—both with round-the-clock security."

Wow. Melanie couldn't help but be impressed. She'd never taken the grand tour of Townsend Acres, but she remembered Christina telling her what an incredible place it was. And it *would* be great to get away from all the hassles.

Melanie eyed him suspiciously. "And what do *you* get in return?" she asked as she continued walking Image toward the barn. "I know you're not offering this out of the goodness of your heart."

"Why, Melanie!" He pressed his palm against his chest, an expression of mock hurt on his face. "You wound me with your harsh words." Then he chuckled. "Actually, I *will* benefit from having Image at Townsend Acres."

"Gee, why am I not surprised?" Melanie couldn't believe she was speaking so bluntly to an adult. But she wanted to be absolutely sure that his offer was straightforward. There was no way she'd even consider moving Image to his farm if he had some shady deal in mind.

Just then Dani came from the barn carrying a cooling sheet and halter. She eyed Brad as if he were an alien before saying to Melanie, "I'll walk her for you until you're finished talking to Mr. Townsend."

"Thanks, Dani. I'll only be a minute or two." Melanie handed the reins to the groom, then faced Brad, her expression skeptical.

"I'll be honest with you," he stated, his tone serious.

Honest? Melanie arched one brow. She wasn't sure Brad Townsend knew the meaning of the word. But if Parker was behind the suggestion, perhaps it was legitimate.

"Ashleigh and Mike may not relish the publicity, and no wonder." He waved his arm around, indicating the farm. "This is no showplace." Melanie opened her mouth to protest, but Brad continued. "Townsend Acres, however, *is* large enough and modern enough to handle publicity."

"Ah. Now I understand." Melanie crossed her arms in front of her chest. Ever since Janice Hart's announcement to the world, Townsend Acres and Celtic Mist had disappeared from the news. Brad obviously hadn't been keeping a low profile by choice. "You're tired of Star and Image getting top billing."

Brad's smile was crafty. "Let's just say that some people are able to use the media to their own advantage."

"And Image stabled at Townsend Acres would certainly turn the spotlight back on you."

"Correct."

For a second Melanie held the man's gaze. His own didn't waver, and she decided that, for once, he was telling the truth. "Let me check with Jazz."

"Already done. Your rock singer thought it was an excellent idea."

Melanie dropped her arms. "What?"

"Parker talked to him early this morning. My son wanted to clear the idea with him before I proposed it to you."

Melanie didn't know whether to feel betrayed or not.

Brad held up both hands, palms out. "Don't get all mad. Jazz said the decision was up to you."

"Well, okay, but I still have to discuss it with Mike and Ashleigh."

"Fine." Brad nodded once. "But don't expect them to be supportive. They'll point out every negative, every flaw in the idea. After all, they want what's best for Christina and Star, *not* you and Image. So when you talk to them, keep in mind what I've offered— peace, security, and four-star accommodations for you *and* your horse. There's even a room and bath in the guest cottage for your dad and his wife." He pointed a finger at her. "So call me as soon as you've made a decision, and I'll send over my van." Then he strode away.

Melanie watched him leave, her thoughts a jumbled mess. Was he right about Ashleigh and Mike? The feud between the Townsends and Griffens went way back. Of course they'd be suspicious of Brad's motives. *She* was suspicious. But it was just for one week, Jazz liked the idea, and—she had to face it—she really had no other options.

Just then Melanie spotted Ashleigh and Mike walking to the mare and foal barn. Their heads were together as if they were deep in conversation.

Better talk to them now. She hurried over, taking off her helmet as she went. "Morning. Do you two have a minute?"

"Sure, Melanie." Ashleigh gave her a pleasant smile.

"What's up?" Mike asked.

"Um, Brad Townsend was here."

"We saw his car." Mike nodded in the direction of the parking area beside the training barn. "We were wondering what he was up to."

"Well, he . . ." Melanie hesitated. Dropping her head, she stared at her paddock boots. Why was she so afraid to tell them about Brad's plan? "Parker came up with a solution to our—to *my* problems."

"Oh?" Ashleigh and Mike glanced at each other, then back at Melanie.

Quickly Melanie told them everything. When she was finished, Ashleigh said, "I think it's an excellent idea. Now, if you'll excuse me, I've got to check on the Walters' broodmare." With a brief smile, she headed to the barn.

Melanie was so astonished by her aunt's reaction, her mouth fell open. Was Ashleigh really *that* eager to get rid of her?

"What about getting to school?" Mike asked.

"Parker can take me in the morning on his way to Whisperwood."

"You'll be okay in an apartment, alone?"

Melanie flushed. Any other time she'd find her uncle's questions annoyingly fatherly. Now she was grateful—it showed *somebody* cared. "Of course, Uncle Mike. You forget I used to be a New Yorker. Besides, I'll only be alone until Dad and Susan arrive."

"True." He smiled. "But you still need to ask your father, and I'll have to inspect your living arrangements. Although since it's the Townsends, I'm sure they're first-class. So plush, you won't want to come back here." Putting his arm around her shoulder, Mike gave her an awkward hug.

Melanie bit her lip to hold back her emotions. "That would never happen, Uncle Mike. No matter what, Whitebrook will always be my home."

When the van carrying Image arrived at Townsend Acres, it was met by two uniformed security guards at the front gate. One guard checked the driver's ID, then waved them through. The press were already waiting. Amazed, Melanie stared out the passenger-side window. Brad stood on the front porch of his southern-style brick mansion, speaking to a barrage of reporters. Lavinia Townsend, his wife, stood beside him, clinging to his arm and smiling winsomely. The reporters turned in unison when the van rumbled past, but Brad soon commandeered their attention again.

The driver continued down a shaded lane. Freshly painted white board fences crisscrossed the blue-green fields. They passed four barns built in a semicircle, beautifully landscaped with flowering azaleas and dogwood trees. Pastures dotted with mares and foals surrounded the barns. Gardens of daffodils and early tulips adorned the walks and entrances. And everywhere there were guards and workers.

"Those four barns are just for mares and foals?" Melanie asked Tony, the driver.

He nodded. "The farm gets mares from all over the world, so we breed even into the summer. That means some mares foal in the late summer."

As the truck roared past one field, a small herd of gorgeous yearlings raced alongside them, separated only by a fence. Beyond the pasture, Melanie glimpsed the training track, which was shaded by tall oaks.

"That's the stallion barn," Tony said, pointing left.

Melanie craned her neck to see past him. The stallion barn was as large as Whitebrook's training barn. It was brick with white trim and located behind the Townsends' mansion, separated from their terraced swimming pool by a grove of trees and a lake. Ten large paddocks surrounded the barn. A few had horses in them.

Every barn, fence, horse, bush, and tree is perfectly groomed, Melanie thought. She and Christina used to joke that each blade of grass at Townsend Acres was trimmed to exactly the same length. But she had to admit that the overall effect was impressive.

"That's Mr. Townsend's most recent addition," Tony continued as he pointed to a medium-sized brick building. The back of the building had four stall doors opening into shaded paddocks. The front of the building, however, looked like a bank or office. "That's the Townsend Horse Center, the farm's own medical facility. Mr. T hired Dr. James Dalton. He's the farm's full-time veterinarian. Does surgery and everything right here on the farm. The building even connects to the therapeutic pool."

They drove past the medical facility, and Melanie wondered where the driver was taking them. Then they took a right and circled clockwise around the training track. On the other side, hidden by the oak trees, was a cottage painted yellow with a darker shade of gingerbread trim. Beside it was a matching barn with its own paddock.

Melanie blinked. It looked like an exclusive resort. "This is where I'm staying?"

The driver chuckled. "Pretty nice, huh? Mr.

Townsend built it for the sheiks, kings, and just plain old millionaires who visit. The barn and cottage have everything a guest needs, whether horse or human."

"Wow," Melanie said again. Image had been deceptively quiet, probably because Baby was along, but as soon as the van parked, she began banging the van floor. "I think Image is eager to try out her new accommodations."

Tony helped Melanie unload the filly. She plunged down the van ramp, whinnying for Baby, who daintily minced down the ramp after her. They turned the horses out in the paddock, two acres of lush grass with an automatic waterer. Tony showed her around the barn, pointing out the amenities, including its own wash area and heated or air-conditioned tack room. He also pointed out the security cameras.

"One is aimed at the stall, another at the barn door, two others at the paddock. The monitor is inside the cottage. You can watch your filly day and night. She'll also be watched by the security guards over the main monitors. So she'll be safe even when you're not around." He handed her the key to the cottage and went to unload the hay, grain, and supplements they'd brought from Whitebrook.

When Melanie was satisfied that Image was happily settled, she headed to the cottage. Tony called good-bye, the van rumbled down the drive, and Melanie stood on the porch, suddenly realizing how quiet it was. There was no Christina blasting music in the bedroom next door. No Kevin clomping into the kitchen. No Ashleigh and Mike discussing horses in the office.

A shiver raced up her spine. Melanie couldn't remember the last time she'd stayed anywhere by herself.

You can handle it, she quickly told herself. Besides, Mike was coming by any minute to bring her suitcase. Turning, Melanie put the key in the lock and opened the door. Slowly it swung wide, and she went inside. It was like going back in time to Victorian days. Melanie peered into the living room—the parlor, she corrected herself. It was furnished with ornate mahogany wing chairs, an overstuffed velour sofa, a whatnot filled with bric-a-brac, and doilies on the chair arms. She continued down the hall to the kitchen, which also looked old-fashioned. But when she opened what looked like an antique icebox, inside was a modern refrigerator stocked with eggs, fruit, juice, cheese, and yogurt—everything Melanie liked to eat.

"Melanie!"

Melanie heard footsteps on the porch. "I'm back here."

Seconds later Mike and Parker came striding down the hallway carrying her things.

Mike whistled. "Hey, a pretty nice pad."

Parker set Melanie's suitcase on the floor and

glanced around. "This *is* nice. I wonder why old Pop hasn't let me stay here."

"Haven't you been here before?" Melanie asked. Parker had a chilly relationship with his father, and much to Brad's dismay, his son avoided the farm business.

"I snooped around when the cottage was first built. But that was before Mom got carte blanche to decorate," he explained as he poked around the kitchen, opening cupboard doors and turning knobs. "Look at this—a microwave hidden in this old-fashioned bread box."

"Where do you want these things, Melanie?" Mike held up her carry bag and pillow.

"Upstairs, I guess," Melanie said, heading down the hall. Before she went upstairs, she peeked into the room opposite the parlor. It was a modern office/den with a big-screen TV, PlayStation, computer, and four-screen security monitor. When Melanie turned it on, she immediately spotted Image and Baby in the pasture.

"Boy, those Victorians were sure inventive," Parker said with a chuckle.

The three went upstairs. The bedrooms were just as cute. A vase of fresh flowers sat on the oak bedside table. A quilt covered the thick mattress on the wrought-iron bed. There was even a replica of an old phone. "Your mom thought of everything," Melanie told Parker after Mike put her things on the bed and went back downstairs. "Thank you. For *everything*."

"Hey, what are friends for?" Parker said. Melanie was glad she still had *one* friend.

Twenty minutes later, Mike and Parker said goodbye. Melanie was sorry to see them go.

"Accommodations approved," Mike said as he kissed the top of her head. "Especially the security part. Now, are you going to be all right?"

Melanie gave him a big smile. "Of course! This is perfect!" She escorted them down the steps and waved as they got into Mike's truck. "Come visit anytime," she called. "And bring Christina and Ashleigh and Kevin and—oh, and Parker, don't forget to pick me up tomorrow morning."

"I won't," Parker called back. Then the truck was heading down the driveway, and Melanie was suddenly alone at Townsend Acres—*the home of the enemy*, she thought. With a heavy heart, she trudged back into the house, reminding herself that Jazz, Susan, and her dad would soon be there.

Plopping down in front of the security monitor, Melanie watched Image as she thought back over the past weeks. Since the Ashland Stakes, she'd lost the good relationship she'd had with Christina and Ashleigh, two of the people she loved the most. And she'd left the only home she'd had for five years. Would either be the same again? On the screen, Image raised her head, trotted over to the fence, and whinnied at some faraway horse. Then she dropped her head to eat.

Melanie's heart lifted. *Image is safe and content,* she told herself. And with the Derby in one week, that was all that mattered.

9

"MORNING, MS. GRAHAM." THE EXERCISE BOY TOUCHED his whip to his helmet. "We're glad to see you at Town-send Acres. I'm quite a fan of your filly. Let me know if you need any help."

Melanie's brows rose under her helmet. "Thanks for the offer."

It was early Monday morning, and Melanie was riding Image around Townsend Acres' training track with half a dozen other horses and riders. The new surroundings seemed to excite the filly. She pranced, blew, and kicked. But none of the other exercise riders seemed to mind her antics. As they steered their mounts around Image, each one greeted Melanie cheerfully and respectfully, their voices touched with a hint of awe.

105

Melanie was amazed. Their attitudes were so different from those of everyone at Whitebrook, where things had been so terribly strained lately. And it wasn't just the morning works that were better. The night before, despite being alone, Melanie had slept like a log. It was the first night in a week she hadn't worried about Image, reporters, or the tensions at the farm. In the morning she'd come downstairs to find a housekeeper preparing a healthy breakfast of fruits and an omelet. So far, being at Townsend Acres was like a vacation.

With a toss of her head, Image broke into a bouncy jig. "Well, not totally a vacation," Melanie told the filly. "I still have *you* and your tantrums to deal with."

Melanie pulled Image's head up and squeezed her into a collected canter, hoping to contain the filly's high spirits. As she cantered counterclockwise around the homestretch turn, she noticed a group of people converging on the track. The crowd was moving alongside a handsome gray ridden by an exercise rider. It was Celtic Mist, Melanie realized, with Brad and at least a dozen reporters walking alongside the colt. As she rode closer, Melanie saw camera flashes go off and heard several shouted questions. *Well, Brad, you got your publicity.*

As the rider jogged Mist clockwise onto the track, Brad caught Melanie's eye, then abruptly turned back to face the reporters. As she cantered down the straightaway, she heard snatches of words, including the names Celtic Mist and Perfect Image. Was Brad comparing the two? Had he purposely brought Mist to the track at the same time as Image? Not that Melanie cared. Mist was a first-class colt, she knew. She'd seen him race before and was impressed with the colt's size, balance, and muscle.

But a Derby-winning Thoroughbred had to have more than physical prowess. *She* needed stamina, intelligence, and heart. "And you've got buckets of all three," Melanie murmured.

Suddenly the sound of pounding hooves made her glance over her shoulder. Celtic Mist was galloping along the inside rail toward them.

Melanie's stomach tightened. The rider was going much faster than Image. When the colt raced past, she didn't know if she could hold the filly. Image's ears flattened, and as the hoofbeats thundered closer, she fought the bit. "Don't you dare," Melanie said, her tone calm. "Brad knows how volatile you are. He knows you hate to get beaten. He *wants* you to go after Mist in front of all those reporters. He wants to stir up trouble. "

Image's ears flicked, her neck arched, and foam flew from her mouth as she worried the bit. "Easy, girl," Melanie crooned, her shoulders and arms aching with the effort of keeping the filly under control. Seconds later Mist blew past.

Image kicked out in protest, but she didn't take off after him. By the time Mist was around the back-side turn, the filly had settled into a reluctant but relaxed trot. Melanie cast a quick look over her shoulder. Brad was staring in her direction. She couldn't see his expression, but his fists were propped on his hips as if he wasn't too happy with the way things had gone. *You just can't have* everything *you want*, Melanie wanted to tell him.

When she reached the far side of track, she walked Image along the outside rail to cool her, deliberately staying away from the group by the gate. Fortunately, there was a gap in the railing and a tanbark-covered path that led to her private barn and cottage.

As she walked over to the gap, a dark-haired kid bustled onto the track to meet her. He had a cooling sheet over one arm and a lead line in his hand. "I take your filly, Ms. Graham," he said with a Spanish accent as he caught hold of Image's bridle.

"Thank you, but I—"

He shook his head vehemently. "No, no. Mr. Townsend insist I be your groom. He say do not take no from the lady."

Melanie glanced suspiciously at the kid. What was Brad trying to pull now? Why would he insist on one of his grooms helping her?

"Well, I'm sorry, but you'll have to tell Mr. Townsend that I take care—" Melanie stopped. The kid had a pained expression on his face and kept glancing across the track toward Brad. "Are you going to get in trouble if you don't groom for me?"

He shifted nervously from foot to foot before whispering, "I get fired."

"Oh." Melanie dismounted. The boy hardly looked dangerous. Maybe Brad *was* just trying to help her out. It was almost impossible for one person to take care of a horse in training, especially since she had to go to school.

Only the kid was so small, Melanie figured Image would eat him for lunch. But when the filly bared her teeth to bite him, he deftly avoided her. At the same time, he crooned to her in Spanish. To Melanie, it sounded like a song. She wasn't sure what Image heard, but the filly must have liked it. She scratched her itchy face on the boy's shoulder, then butted him affectionately. She even stood still while he draped the cooler over her haunches.

Melanie was totally amazed. "What's your name?" she asked as they walked together down the path.

"Marcos."

"Have you been working with horses a long time, Marcos?"

"Long time in Mexico. Two weeks in United States." He frowned seriously. "Pay much better here. I send money home to help my family."

Melanie arched one brow. Marcos looked about

fourteen, hardly old enough to support a family. "So, Marcos, did Mr. Townsend give you any special instructions?" *Like to poison Image's feed?*

He puffed out his skinny chest. "He just say the filly *mucho* important and to take good care of her."

Melanie eyed him. She didn't trust many people to take care of Image, but she also didn't want Marcos to get fired. Perhaps he could keep an eye on Image while she was at school.

School. Melanie checked her watch. She was running late. The night before, she'd studied for the last chemistry test of the grading period. Being away from Whitebrook had somehow made it easier to concentrate. She had to get at least a B on it to pass for this six-week period, but she felt as if she knew the material—for once.

As Melanie hurried down the path beside Marcos and Image, she shook her head. A week before the Derby and she was worrying about chemistry and high school. She doubted any of the other jockeys or trainers had such stupid problems. But she was determined to handle them. Image's workouts since the Ashland Stakes had been super. And things were already looking up since they'd moved to Townsend Acres. Image was fit, happy, and ready to race a mile and a half against colts.

But to win the Derby, Melanie reminded herself, she needed to be equally as ready.

● ● ●

"Susan! Dad! I'm so glad to see you!" Melanie called when they came through the security checkpoint at the airport. Flinging herself into her father's arms, she gave him a huge hug. Then she pecked her stepmother on the cheek.

"Wow, what a reception," her father said. Melanie grinned at him. Will Graham looked New York handsome. His salt-and-pepper hair was styled long, and he wore casual but expensive clothes. Susan looked fashionable as well in a silk blouse and linen slacks. Melanie genuinely liked her stepmother, although they hadn't spent much time together.

"Where's Jazz?" Melanie asked, casting a worried glance behind them. "Didn't he come with you?"

Will chuckled. "Don't panic. Several fans in the gangway accosted him. I just hope he survives with his clothes and hair intact. The fans looked determined to get a souvenir."

Melanie took a bag from Susan. "Here, let me help. You'll never guess how we're getting to Townsend Acres. *Limo*. Brad sent me over here with his limousine and special driver." She giggled. "He said that Jazz and I were such celebrities, he wanted us to be safe."

Will gave Susan an uncomfortable look.

"And he's invited us all to his Derby blowout tonight, and if we want, he's arranged for us to ride on

111

the *Belle of Louisville* in the steamboat race. Can you believe it? That honor is usually reserved for dignitaries!" Melanie exclaimed, but then she saw Jazz hurrying toward the security checkpoint, and she waved excitedly. "Jazz!"

As always, he looked terrific in spite of his unusual getup. He wore wire-rimmed glasses, pressed khakis, and a button-down striped shirt with a pocket protector. In one hand he carried a laptop. She laughed when he came up. "Is this your geek disguise?" she teased as she plucked a pen from his pocket.

"Actually, this is what I really look like," he said, returning her grin. "Didn't I mention that I was a nerd at Central High?"

"No, but that's fine with me," Melanie replied, a rush of emotions filling her. She was amazed at how much she'd missed him. "I like you even if you are an egghead."

"That's nice to hear." He took a step toward her, his gaze intense, his smile soft. Melanie searched his eyes. Had he missed her as much?

"A-hem." Will cleared his throat, and Melanie sprang away from Jazz. "When you two are ready, we'll head down to get our baggage."

"We're ready!" Melanie exclaimed. Bustling forward, she led the way down the aisle. "The limo's parked right out front. It will take us directly to Townsend Acres. Brad's party starts at seven. He's having a hundred guests! It's a huge pig roast with all the mint juleps you can drink."

"Is there time in our busy schedule to see Mike and Ashleigh?" Susan asked.

"They'll be at Brad's bash, too," Melanie explained. "Wait until you see the guest cottage where I've been staying. Where *you'll* be staying. And Image . . ." Melanie turned and walked backward a second. "Image is positively thriving. She has a new groom, Marcos, who—"

"A new groom! What about me?" Jazz gasped with mock dismay.

Melanie laughed. "She still loves you, Jazz, don't worry. But Marcos is terrific—the first groom she hasn't tried to kill. Last night he slept on a cot in the barn. He said it was because he wanted to watch over Image. But I think the barn's more comfortable than the bunkhouse where he usually sleeps."

As they stopped by the baggage carousel, Will took her hand in his. "Melanie, you sound breathless with happiness. That's a big difference from when we talked last weekend. But are you sure this arrangement with Brad is legitimate?"

"Oh, Dad, I know it sounds funny, since Brad has always been the enemy, but moving to Townsend Acres was the best decision that I—that *we*"—she nodded at Jazz—"ever made. You have no idea how tense things had become at Whitebrook. And the security at

Townsend Acres is incredible. I don't lie awake nights wondering if someone is going to mess with Image. Plus everyone at the farm has been so nice."

Will still didn't look convinced. "Melanie, last time I was here, Brad and I were fighting for control of Image. You were determined that he wouldn't get his hands on her. Now he's got you and her on his farm, and he's treating you both like princesses. It's just hard for me not to be suspicious."

"I understand exactly where you're coming from," she agreed. "I was suspicious, too. But Brad told me what he was getting out of the deal—publicity. And it's worked. This morning's sports page was filled with articles on Celtic Mist, whom Brad just moved to Churchill Downs, and Image. Star wasn't mentioned, so the reporters must be leaving Whitebrook alone, which should make Christina and Ashleigh happy."

Jazz faced Will. "I think Melanie's right. Parker had a hand in the idea, too, and I don't think he'd have anything to do with it if Brad was going to pull a fast one. Besides, I signed a business contract that he faxed me. Staying at Townsend Acres is not free, you know." He chuckled. "That's why I have to play all these concerts—to support my horse."

Everybody laughed, and Will's tight expression relaxed. Melanie understood her father's concerns. Brad *was* the enemy, and that would never change. But she also knew how much better things were at

Townsend Acres. She loved the Reeses, and she knew that they loved her, but their close relationship had only made things worse when she'd decided to enter Image in the Derby. It was tough to compete against someone you cared about.

Susan touched Will on the arm. "Okay, *Dad*," she said, her tone teasing. "I think your daughter knows what she's doing."

"Well, *that's* a first," he replied with mock gruffness, and everybody laughed again.

After they retrieved the luggage, Melanie led them to the limousine. They piled into the luxurious interior—Will and Susan on one side, Jazz and Melanie facing them. On the way to Townsend Acres, the four talked nonstop. Jazz described his last concert, Will and Susan discussed Graham Productions and the latest rock group they'd signed, and Melanie handed her dad her report card for the past six weeks. Her father took his time opening it. His eyes widened in mock horror.

"Is it that bad?" Susan asked hesitantly.

Looking up at Melanie, Will grinned. "No, it's that good. Congratulations, sweetie." He leaned forward and gave her a kiss on the cheek. "You brought your chemistry and English grades up."

Jazz twisted around, trying to read the grades. "Looks like the only way chemistry could have gone *was* up," he said dryly.

"Hey, I worked hard for that grade," Melanie protested. "I got an A on my makeup quiz, thanks to Parker, who's been helping me study."

"We're proud of you," Will said.

"Thanks, Dad." Melanie clapped her hands together excitedly. "And now I'm ready to celebrate. Tonight there's Brad's party, tomorrow there's the Pegasus Parade in downtown Louisville, and Friday there's the Kentucky Oaks."

"How about time to see my favorite racehorse?" Jazz asked.

"The Townsends' Derby bash doesn't start until seven. *Evening attire*," Melanie said, imitating Lavinia's voice. "So we'll have time to see Image, meet Marcos, and shower and dress. I even bought a new outfit!"

"You sound excited about going," Will said.

"I'm excited about *everything*." Reaching over, Melanie clasped her father's hands in hers. Her eyes gleamed. "Ever since Jazz and I first talked about entering Image in the Derby, I've been worried about the race. But I don't feel that way anymore. I feel confident that Image *can* win. And do you know what that means? She'll be the fourth filly in history to win. Millions will watch us on TV. We'll be written up in every newspaper. Dad, if we win, we'll be legends!"

10

"Jazz, look, that's Prince Mohammad Abdul from Saudi Arabia," Melanie whispered. "He's the owner of War Ghost. Guess what his racing colors are?" Jazz and Melanie were standing by the side of the Townsends' pool. Heads together, they watched the owners, trainers, and jockeys stream through the entryway and onto the patio for Brad and Lavinia's Derby bash.

"Silver and gold," Jazz whispered back.

"How did you guess?"

"I've been reading the sports pages, too," he said. "The prince and War Ghost have gotten their photo in the paper quite a bit. Besides, what other colors would a billionaire prince choose?"

Melanie giggled. "True." She was wearing her new

short-sleeved silk dress in fire engine red splashed with blue and yellow. The neck was scooped low and the hem was at midthigh. When she lived in New York, all her clothes had been fashionably edgy. But since she'd been at Whitebrook, she'd worn pretty much nothing but jeans and paddock boots. That evening when she'd gotten dressed, though, she'd realized how much fun it was to wear wild clothes again. Jazz, however, was dressed incognito in a navy blue suit and light blue shirt. His only concession to fashion was no tie and Docksiders worn with no socks.

Suddenly Melanie gasped, "Oh, my gosh! There's Bob Baffert! He's like the king of horse racing. Do you think I could get his autograph?"

Jazz laughed. "Why not?" He grinned as he checked out all the partiers. "You know, I kind of like being the object of *no* attention. Not one person here has given me a second look."

"Why would they, when all these real celebrities are here?" Melanie teased. "Even Will and Susan found some millionaire horse owner to chat up. That's Lily Hammer, owner and CEO of Hammer Advertising. Hammer Advertising wrote all the TV ads publicizing the Derby. Lily Hammer also owns TV Time, one of the Derby entries. Colt's never won a race, so no one's too worried about him." Melanie's eyes widened. "Hey, isn't that Rory McNaught, the owner of Derry O'Dell? This spring he brought his colt to the United

118

States from Dublin. Last month Derry was second in the Wood Memorial."

"I remember reading about him. The colt might be tough to beat."

"Mmm," Melanie mumbled, although she really wasn't paying attention. She was too busy staring in amazement at the star-studded cast of Derby players who'd been invited to the Townsends'. Owners, jockeys, trainers, Churchill Downs track officials, and Kentucky dignitaries were already clustered on the lawn, on the patio, and around the pool, and more kept arriving. The tiered stone patio was decorated to the hilt with vases full of red roses on every table. As soon as Melanie and Jazz arrived, a server had handed them nonalcoholic mint juleps. They hadn't had time to inspect the food, which was arranged on silver platters on horseshoe-shaped tables decorated with ice sculptures of previous Derby winners, but Melanie knew that the Townsends served only the best.

"Ready to get something to eat?" Jazz asked. "The last thing I had was pretzels on the plane, and I think I see shrimp over there. And are those crab legs?"

"Wait, look who's coming in." Melanie tugged on his coat sleeve. "Fusao Tsuge. He's the Japanese guy who bought Ingleside after the colt won the Illinois Derby. He bought him for two million just so he'd have a horse to race in the Kentucky Derby!"

"Man, it would be nice to have that kind of money to

plop down on a horse anytime you wanted," Jazz said as he sipped his icy mint drink. "Hey, isn't that Christina Reese behind him?" he suddenly gasped, his voice filled with mock awe. "You know, the owner of Wonder's Star, possible Derby winner? And look who she's with— Olympic rider Parker Townsend, son of Brad and Lavinia Townsend, social climbers extraordinaire."

Melanie laughed. Jazz had perfectly parodied her reverent tone. "Possible Derby winner?" She shook her head. "I don't think so. That title is reserved for Image." She nudged Jazz. "Christina and Parker do look cute together. Did you know she asked him to the senior prom?"

"I thought they'd broken up."

"They had, but I think things are heating up again between them." Melanie watched the two together. As they made their way through the crowd, Parker had his hand on Christina's elbow. Her cousin looked especially cute in a sapphire-blue sheath and strappy high heels.

"Let's go hang out with them," Jazz said, starting toward the couple.

Catching his hand, Melanie drew him back. "Not yet. Christina and I haven't been exactly best buds lately. In fact, I haven't talked to her since I moved out."

Jazz gave her a surprised look. "You haven't? That was days ago. Don't you see her at school?"

"We don't have any classes together, so I've been able to avoid her."

Jazz continued to stare at her. "Mel, you and Chris have got to resolve this feud before the race. Remember, you've been friends way longer than you've been competitors."

Melanie grimaced. "Tell *her* that. She's the one who's been in a huff."

He threw up his hands. "All right. Don't make up. But I'm going over to talk to them. They're both still *my* friends." He took off without a backward glance.

"That's what you think," Melanie muttered under her breath. Eyes on Jazz, she moseyed over to one of the food tables, pretending to be interested in the variety of party foods. She wished Jazz hadn't stridden off so quickly. She would have explained to him why it was so hard for her to talk to Christina. She'd asked herself a hundred times what she could say that would make things right. But the one thing Christina wanted was the one thing Melanie couldn't do for her. *I love you, cuz, but not enough to withdraw Image from the Derby.*

Melanie glanced toward the entryway. She wondered if Ashleigh and Mike had arrived yet. And if they had, what would she say to her aunt and uncle? *I miss you, but I'm having the time of my life at Townsend Acres.* Melanie sighed. She picked up a strawberry dipped in chocolate and popped it in her mouth.

Just then Dustin Gates, Speed.com's owner, and Alexis Huffman walked in. Melanie almost choked on the strawberry. Alexis's arm was linked with Dustin's, and she stared adoringly up at him.

Well, congratulations, Alexis, Melanie thought snidely. *You snagged a Derby contender* and *its owner.*

Following behind them were Cindy McLean and Ben al-Rihani. So far, it appeared that Brad and Lavinia had invited every owner of every Derby entry. To impress them and gloat? That would be typical Brad behavior.

"Hello, Melanie. I'm glad you made it to the party." Brad came up beside her, a plate in his hand, his gaze on a platter of crab-stuffed mushrooms. "Are your dad and Susan enjoying their accommodations?"

"Definitely. They couldn't stop talking about the cottage," Melanie said sincerely. "Thank you for inviting them. It was very generous of you."

"My pleasure." Brad gave her a warm smile. "You know, I vaguely remember a very different conversation we had at a similar party."

"The Freedmans'," Melanie said. How could she forget it? She could recall Brad's every word: *Image will never win a race.* "Great party, although it wasn't quite as lavish as yours."

"Ah, yes. The Freedmans try to outdo us every

year. But they never succeed. Like you," he added smoothly.

Melanie cast a sharp look at him. "Pardon me?"

"Granted, Image has done much better than I thought," Brad said as he reached for a tiny appetizer to add to his plate. "But don't fool yourself into thinking she's going to win Saturday."

"*Fool* myself?" Melanie repeated, keeping her tone as smooth as his. "No, you can be sure I'm not fooling myself. As I recall, at the Freedmans' party you also told me I'd never make it as a trainer. And that Image would never make it as a racehorse. Well, you were wrong then, and I bet you're wrong this time, too. Image has as good a chance to win the Derby as any colt."

Brad arched one brow and turned to face her. "I'm not a gambling man, Melanie, but I'll take that bet. Simply because there's not one chance in a million that Image can win."

"So what are we betting?" Melanie declared.

Suddenly Melanie heard a gasp. She swung around. Christina was standing stiffly behind her. Her expression told Melanie that she'd overheard their conversation. "Excuse me, Mr. Townsend," Christina said. "I need to talk to my cousin about—about *school*." Grabbing Melanie by the arm, Christina dragged her away from Brad.

"Melanie, what are you doing?" her cousin hissed. "Making a bet with Brad? *Are you crazy?*"

"No, I'm not crazy." Melanie yanked her arm from Christina's grasp. "And what business is it of yours?"

Christina scowled. "What business? You have to ask me that?" She waved her hand toward Brad, who was already talking to someone else. "After all the stories Ashleigh's told you? After the almost-fiasco I had with him and Star? After he ruined Fredericka so she'd be forced to sell Image to him?"

Melanie bit her lip. "Okay, okay, you're right. I was momentarily crazed." She clenched her fists by her side. "But I'm so sick of people telling me that Image will never win."

"That's no reason to make a bet with Brad," Christina said. "He'd try to win your soul if he could."

She said it so seriously that Melanie began to giggle. "Thanks for saving me, then. I'd like to hang on to my soul."

"No problem." Christina smiled cautiously. "I needed an excuse to talk to you, anyway. I've been kind of avoiding you. It was hard to know what to say since I got angry at you the other day. But when I came over and heard Brad say he'd make a bet with you, I knew I'd better say something fast."

"I'm glad you came over," Melanie admitted. "I wanted to talk to you, too, but I was kind of afraid. You *have* been acting pretty angry and standoffish lately."

"Me?" Christina seemed startled. "How about you?

Disappearing Sunday without even a good-bye. Then I find out you're staying *here*."

"Where else was I going to go?" Melanie asked. "You and Ashleigh could barely stand having me at Whitebrook."

Christina put her hands on her hips. "You mean *you* could barely stand to be around *us!*" she corrected. "Like you and Image the superfilly are too important to be in the same room with us."

Melanie's jaw dropped.

"Actually, I wasn't surprised when you came to Townsend Acres, where even the horses have servants," Christina continued, her cheeks flushing pink. "Since you and Image have become pampered celebrities, Whitebrook obviously wasn't good enough for you."

"*That's* why you think we're here?" Melanie gasped.

"Yes," Christina said almost coldly. "That's one reason. The other reason you left is because when things got tense at Whitebrook, you couldn't handle it. No one asked you to leave, Melanie. You ran away from New York when things got tough. Now you're running away from us. Well, relationships in families don't always go smoothly, but that's no reason to run away." With those last words, Christina picked up her plate and hurried into the crowd of partygoers.

No, that's not the reason! Melanie wanted to call after her. *I left because I didn't want Image to get hurt!* But she couldn't get out the words. Dropping her drink on the table, Melanie hurried from the tables of food and the swarm of people. She passed by a group standing poolside, talking together. The group included Cindy and Ben.

"Perfect Image?" she heard someone say. "Too unpredictable. And her rider's just a kid. They'll crash and burn." Ears stinging, Melanie fled in the other direction to the fence that separated the lake from the backyard. Leaning on the top rail, she gazed across the acres of rolling fields and tried to hold back the tears.

Was Brad right? Was Melanie fooling herself into thinking that Image had a chance at the Derby?

And was Christina right? Had Melanie run away when things became too tough?

No, that isn't why. Melanie shook her head. *Christina's just mad. And Brad's his usual egotistical self. The Derby's four days away, and everybody's on edge.* No matter how bizarre it must seem to Christina, Melanie was happy at Townsend Acres, and Image was thriving. For the next few days Melanie needed to quit worrying about what everybody else thought. She needed to focus solely on preparing Image for the Derby. *And winning.*

11

Saturday morning.

Derby day.

Melanie woke at five o'clock. There was so much to do!

She leaped out of bed, humming with nervous excitement. She'd managed to sleep about five hours—a miracle, really, considering how wound up everybody was. She'd stayed up until midnight playing cards with Will, Jazz, and Susan. Earlier they'd been at Churchill Downs, watching the fillies race in the Kentucky Oaks. Wave Dancer, the filly who had tried to gain on Image in the Ashland Stakes, had won.

Of course, if Image had been racing, she would have won.

Still humming, Melanie grabbed clean underwear

127

and headed into the adjoining shower. When she was finished, she towel-dried her hair. Her stomach growled loudly. Had she remembered to eat the night before? She knew she had to eat this morning. She wasn't worried about making her racing weight. She was, however, worried about keeping up her energy. Riding Image burned lots of calories.

Throwing on a big shirt, she padded into the hall. The doors to the other bedrooms were closed. The cottage was silent. Quietly Melanie tiptoed downstairs and into the kitchen. A reddish gray glow came in through the bay window; otherwise the kitchen was dark. Melanie blinked. Was someone sitting in a kitchen chair? She could see a head silhouetted in the dim light.

"Morning." It was Jazz. "Don't turn on the light. My eyes aren't quite open yet." He was slouched in a chair, bare-chested, wearing baggy cotton pants with a drawstring.

"What are you doing up so early?"

"Couldn't sleep," he said, raising a mug. "So I made some hot chocolate."

"Yum." Melanie padded over to the stove. "Any left?"

He jumped from the chair. "Here, sit down. I'll get you some."

"Thanks. Except I can't sit down. Too wired." Melanie crossed to the refrigerator, conscious of his closeness. Even half asleep, with rumpled hair, Jazz looked cute. "How about I make some breakfast? I need to eat."

"Sounds great. But only if I can help. I make a mean scrambled eggs with salsa."

"Help accepted," Melanie said as she opened the refrigerator door. "I remember those great meals you and the other band members made in Florida."

"But first I want you to open something."

Melanie turned. Jazz stood right behind her, holding a large white box with a poufy bow.

"What's this?"

He grinned. "A present. I've wanted to give it to you a million times since we got here."

Melanie took it from him. "A present?"

"Open it."

Setting the box on the table, Melanie untied the bow and lifted off the top. Heart pounding, she folded back the tissue paper to reveal a silky emerald-green shirt with a pattern of white music notes across the bodice. For a second Melanie didn't understand what she was looking at. Jazz had bought her a shirt? But when she picked it up and saw the helmet cover underneath, it hit her—Jazz had gotten racing silks in his own colors.

"Oh, my gosh!" Melanie exclaimed. "I can't believe it! Image will have her own colors!"

Jazz nodded excitedly. "A month ago I applied to

the Jockey Club and the Kentucky race authority. They approved the colors and the pattern, and I had the shirt and helmet cover made. Do you like the music notes? I thought it was a unique touch."

"I love them!" Melanie beamed at Jazz. "I'll be the only jockey with a song on her shirt. Thank you, Jazz. This is so special."

He grinned sheepishly, as if embarrassed by her thanks. "I thought it was time—now that I'm Image's owner."

Melanie's smile suddenly faded. This would be the first time Image hadn't raced under Whitebrook's colors.

"What's wrong?" Jazz asked quickly.

"I was just wondering what Mike and Ashleigh were going to think."

"Actually, Mike suggested it," Jazz admitted. "He didn't think Star and Image should race in the Derby under the same colors, especially since Whitebrook doesn't own Image."

"Oh." Ducking her head, Melanie folded the shirt and placed it back in the box.

Jazz touched her shoulder. "Mel, this doesn't mean it's the end of your relationship with the Reeses and Whitebrook. It just means that Image deserves her *own* colors. It'll be so cool when those green-and-white colors are the first to flash across the finish line!"

• • •

Later that morning Melanie slipped on the emerald shirt. The silky material felt cool and soft to the touch. For an instant she checked out her image in the mirror over the sink in the women's locker area of the Churchill Downs jockeys' lounge. *You look like a winner,* she thought. Another female jockey came into the room. Flushing, Melanie spun away from the mirror. "Thought I spotted a loose thread," she explained, then immediately wondered why she should be embarrassed.

When she was finally dressed, she picked up her saddle and headed into the main room to get weighed in. She spotted Christina, who was hanging out with Fred and Karen. Her cousin eyed her new shirt, then turned away and resumed her conversation.

Melanie sighed and headed toward the scale room. A group of the older jockeys had surrounded a kid wearing purple-and-green silks. *Tall Oaks colors.* Melanie knew it had to be Wolf, the young exercise rider that Cindy and Ben had riding Gratis. Wolf had almost no experience, but so far he was the only rider who could handle the feisty, aggressive colt. Still, Ben and Cindy were taking a big chance using him.

"Hey, Wolf, get in our way in the Derby and we'll shoot you down like the varmint you are," one of the guys was saying.

131

Melanie stopped. Wolf's dark brows were knitted together and his expression was so fierce, he *looked* like a wolf ready to attack.

"Then we'll run over you like roadkill," the second jockey chimed in. Melanie recognized him. It was Turk Watson, Speed.com's rider. Turk usually rode in New York, but his reputation for rough behavior—on and off the track—had spread to Kentucky.

"Yeah, you ain't even a bug," the third one added. "That means you're below a bug. So that must make you—"

"A lower life form," Melanie cut in. Without thinking, she stepped in between Wolf and the other jockeys. "Which is still higher on the evolutionary scale than you three morons." Behind her, Wolf chuckled quietly.

"Ooooo." Turk pressed his hand to his heart, pretending to be wounded. "The chick is major harsh. Though you'd better save all that negative energy for the Derby. You're going to need it when we spill your guts all over the track."

"Oh, yeah? You old men gotta catch me first," she retorted before pushing past them, their guffaws following her to the scale room. *Now why did I get in the middle of that?* Melanie wondered. Since she'd started racing, she'd had her share of run-ins with other jockeys. But alienating the other jockeys in the race wasn't too smart. She already had enough worries. She was passing by the TV when a still of Image caught her attention. The filly was behind a white board fence and facing the camera, her ears pricked, her eyes wide.

Instantly Melanie recognized the shot. The photo had to have been taken the night she'd chased the intruder out of Image's paddock. So that's what the person had been doing. "And that was Perfect Image, who's made this year's Derby into a contest between one filly and eight colts," the television commentator was saying to the audience. "What do you think, Al?" he asked, holding a microphone up to an older guy. "Do you think this *will* be a contest?"

Melanie vaguely recognized the gray-haired man as one of the network sportscasters who announced the Derby every year. "Well, Don, the hype and publicity certainly have helped interest in the Derby," the man said. "The crowd, estimated at a hundred and sixty thousand, is the largest since it was first run in 1875. Seating capacity is only forty-eight thousand five hundred, so the infield is overflowing. And earlier I interviewed racegoers as they came through the gates. The majority of fans are here to watch history in the making. If Perfect Image wins, she'll be the second filly ridden by a female to win the Derby."

"What chance is there of that happening?" the commentator asked.

Al shrugged. "Perfect Image is no Winning Colors, winner of the 1988 Derby. And certainly Melanie Graham is no Julie Krone or Ashleigh Griffen, who both won jewels of the Triple Crown. So my odds match the odds on the tote board: twenty to one. The crowd may love the filly, but they're not going to bet money on her."

Melanie's face burned. Behind her, the three jockeys she'd just harassed snickered loudly.

Wolf came up to her. "Don't pay attention to the jerks," he said in a low voice, a scowl still on his face.

"Thanks, Wolf, but I'm used to it. You'd better get used to it, too, if you want to be a jockey."

"Don't worry. I've got tough skin." He thumped himself hard on the chest, as if to prove it. Then he sauntered away, glaring at anyone who glanced his way.

I wish I had tough skin, Melanie thought.

Just then Christina came from the locker room. For a second she stared at Melanie as if she wanted to say something. But then she turned away and began watching the television.

Taking a deep breath, Melanie forced herself to walk toward her cousin. She knew what she had to do. "Christina," she said, "I wanted to wish you the best of luck. And I wanted to tell you that no matter what happens, I'll always think of you as my best friend." Quickly she whirled and strode to the scales before

134

Christina could react. *There, I said it. Now I can concentrate on what I need to do. Ride like the wind!*

Melanie caught her breath when Image strutted into the paddock. The filly was absolutely glowing with health and energy.

Marcos walked on one side of her, Jazz on the other. The two had immediately struck up a friendship, and Melanie often caught them discussing horses and grooming like two buddies. She knew they'd spent hours that morning pampering the filly, even fighting for Image's affections. Now they faced front with proud and determined expressions. And they had plenty to be proud of. Neck arched, tail flowing, Image pranced between Marcos and Jazz as if she were the drum majorette leading the marching band. Melanie had to smile. The filly wasn't the least bit nervous. She was truly showing off. As the three walked by a group of girls in the crowd, the girls cheered and held up posters: FILLIES RULE! EAT OUR DUST, COLTS! PERFECT IMAGE—NUMBER ONE FILLY! Ducking her head and shaking it, Image kicked up her heels as if to say, *You got that right.*

Melanie groaned silently, hoping the pomp and adulation wouldn't go to Image's head. The filly certainly looked like a star, and from the reactions of the crowd—the hooting, pointing, and cheering—she *was* the star of the day. "Ms. Graham! Ms. Graham! Sign my race program!" Melanie heard several voices shout from the crowd.

Better not let it go to your head, either, Melanie reminded herself. Since she'd arrived that morning, she'd been besieged with fans until she'd figured out that she had to stay in the secure areas.

Trying to keep out of the limelight, Melanie stepped back into the shadow of Image's saddling stall. As Melanie watched the horses continue their walk around the paddock, she realized how different this was from the parade of fillies in the Ashland Stakes. Derry O'Dell, Celtic Mist, Speed.com, and War Ghost were taller than Image. Ingleside and TV Time were smaller, but compact and athletic like sprinters. Gratis and Wonder's Star were about Image's size, and both had the lean, taut build of a distance runner. And all the three-year-old colts were broader and better-muscled than the fillies, with deep girths and wide chests.

Melanie ticked off the entries as they circled around her. The night before, she'd read their stats and gone over their timed works with Jazz, but this would be her last chance to view them from the ground.

Number one was Ingleside, the Illinois Derby winner, ridden by Dan Waise, a top jockey who was returning for his tenth Derby ride. Number two was Celtic Mist. Emilio Casados, the jockey Brad had hired, had ridden the colt to a win in the Arkansas Derby. Wonder's Star had pulled the number three slot, a good position, and Melanie had no doubt that Christina would be riding to win. Number four was TV Time, another Kentucky-bred horse. TV Time was the most unseasoned, with just three previous starts. But the colt looked good, and Melanie's friend Vicky Frontiere was riding him. Melanie knew that Vicky was a super rider.

Number five was Derry O'Dell, the Irish-bred colt, ridden by an English jockey whom Melanie knew only by his incredible win record. Number six was War Ghost. Prince Abdul had bought the yearling for three million dollars with one goal in mind—winning the Derby. Since Hall of Fame trainer D. Wayne Lukas trained War Ghost, Melanie knew the colt would be a tough contender. Number seven was Speed.com. Dustin Gates had hired Turk Watson, who'd ridden the colt to a win in the Blue Grass Stakes. Image was number eight, and last but not least was number nine, Gratis, Cindy and Ben's colt, ridden by Wolf.

Melanie worried about Image's position in the field. The filly was sandwiched between Gratis, an aggressive colt ridden by a totally inexperienced jockey who was bound to make mistakes, and Speed.com, a fast-breaking colt ridden by an aggressive jockey who hated to lose. Melanie had watched a video of Speed.com in the Blue Grass Stakes. The colt had broken fast, cut in front of the horse beside him, then raced to the finish line, leading wire to wire.

The newscasters were right—this might not be the largest Derby field, but it *was* one of the toughest. Suddenly all the negative comments from the past weeks rose to haunt Melanie: *There's no way Image can win.*

They'll crash and burn.

One chance in a million that Image can win.

Image is no Winning Colors. Melanie Graham is no Julie Krone.

Melanie felt the bottom fall out of her stomach. All her earlier confidence fell with it. She'd been nervous before the Ashland Stakes. Now she was *terrified*.

12

MELANIE CLUTCHED HER STOMACH, SUDDENLY QUEASY AS the horses paraded around her in a dizzy circle. She groaned as the realization hit her. Only Jazz and she had faith in Image. Everyone else thought they would fail.

Then Melanie caught herself. *What's so astonishing about that?* From the beginning, few had thought Image would make it. And so what if the odds were 20 to 1? Melanie also knew the facts. The Derby favorite had won only two times in the last twenty-four years. Charismatic, the 1999 winner, had gone off at 31 to 1. And hadn't the 2002 winner, War Emblem, gone off at 20 to 1, too? Besides, Brad was wrong. Image didn't have one chance in a million to win. She had one chance in nine. All she had to do was beat eight colts. Those were good enough odds for Melanie.

When Marcos and Jazz brought Image toward the saddling stall, Melanie held her head high and met them with a determined look. Marcos had a huge grin on his face.

"First time I lead such a famous horse! All the girls cheer for her," Marcos announced happily as he led Image into the stall. Protesting, Image squealed and tried to back out. Jazz, who was reaching for the saddlecloth and pad, jumped out of her way. Hanging lightly to the lead, Marcos ran backward with her. "She likes the cheering," he told Melanie, still grinning. "And the running and the winning. But not the saddling. Come, sweet señorita," he cajoled until the filly minced back into the stall. Melanie laughed at the pair. Marcos was tiny compared to Image. But he handled her perfectly—pampering her yet at the same time making her listen. They'd even been able to leave Baby at Townsend Acres.

"Do you think you can get this famous horse saddled?" Jazz asked Marcos with a concerned frown.

"Piece of cake, Jazz," Melanie said as she took the pad from him. "Marcos, what's the song you sing to her?"

"'Haga Mi Día.'"

Jazz's brows shot up. "That's 'Make My Day.' I'd forgotten the song was popular in Mexico."

Melanie began to hum the song. Avoiding Image's swishing tail and swinging haunches, she managed to get the filly saddled with Jazz's help. When Melanie tightened the girth, Image hopped in place. Quickly Marcos moved her out for the final inspection.

After Melanie fastened her helmet strap, Jazz slipped his hand into hers. "Do you think the cameras are on us?" he whispered.

"I doubt it. Why?"

Pulling her around, he kissed her softly on the lips. Melanie's mouth parted in surprise. "That's for good luck," he said in a husky voice.

"Do you think the other owners are kissing their jockeys for good luck?" she teased, trying to ignore the hot flush creeping up her neck.

"Riders up!"

The paddock judge's shout made Melanie jump away from Jazz. "This is it," she said, taking a deep breath. Still holding his hand, Melanie hurried over to Image and Marcos.

When the filly stood still for an instant, Jazz boosted her into the saddle. "This *is* it," he repeated as he stepped away and gave her an encouraging smile. "Meet you at the winner's circle!" he called. The plan was for Jazz to change into a white shirt and emerald-green tie, his racing colors. If Image did win, he'd be required to talk to every reporter and pose for every camera.

As Marcos led Image away, Melanie pressed her palm against the filly's shoulder. She could feel the rise and fall of Image's bones and muscles.

"This filly fast, eh?" Marcos asked as they followed the other horses through the tunnel under the Churchill Downs clubhouse.

"Very fast," Melanie murmured.

"And strong?"

"Very strong."

"Then she win. I know. She told me she don't like to lose."

Melanie laughed. She could truly imagine Image and Marcos talking. "That's the truth."

As the horses emerged from the tunnel onto the track, a bugler announced the post parade. Marcos unclipped the lead and stepped back. Image immediately broke into a nervous trot.

"Good luck, Miss Melanie!" he called.

Melanie turned right, following the string of horses as they paraded in front of the clubhouse. The University of Louisville band launched into "My Old Kentucky Home."

Goose bumps of excitement rose on Melanie's arms. She could feel her adrenaline stirring. Bobbing her head and swishing her tail, Image pranced in time to the music. Melanie kept a light hold on the reins. She tried to keep her thoughts just as light. She wanted Image to be able to fly around the track as if she had wings.

The roar of the huge crowd was deafening. People overflowed the stands and the infield. Over the din, the announcer's voice called out the horses' and jockeys' names and their numbers as they circled to again walk past the clubhouse, with its towering twin spires, and the newer grandstand. "Six minutes to go!" the announcer called.

When Melanie was past the grandstand, she leaned forward and Image broke into a smooth canter. Beside her, Gratis fought with Wolf. Directly in front of her, Speed.com strained to get away from his pony horse. When she looked up the track, she caught a glimpse of Star's chestnut coat and Christina's blue-and-white shirt. "Good luck, Chris," Melanie murmured, but then she turned her mind back to Image. *Forget the crowds. Forget the other horses. Focus on Image.*

As they cantered, Melanie held her breath, listening and feeling for any hesitation or bobble in Image's gait. The filly had been sound all week. She'd passed the vet check with flying colors, but the track was rated as fast. That meant the horses would be going at top speed. They'd be putting an incredible strain on their bones and tendons. Melanie wanted to be extra cautious. Fortunately, the filly's stride felt rocking-chair smooth. She turned and trotted Image back to the starting gate, set up at the beginning of the homestretch. The other colts were milling behind it. As she waited to load, Melanie tuned out the announcer, who kept up a running commentary. She tuned out the other horses and jockeys, circling around the gate. She tuned out the blue-shirted starters and assistants, and the crush of whistling and cheering watchers in the infield.

And she tuned out the nerves zinging through her.

This was the historic Kentucky Derby. The Run for the Roses. The first jewel of the Triple Crown. It would be televised all over the world. The next day it would be in every newspaper.

It was also the greatest race of Melanie's life. But none of that mattered.

The only thing that mattered was one horse, Image, running her heart out, giving everything in her quest to be the first over the finish line. All week Melanie had agonized over strategy. Should she try to lead wire to wire, as in the Ashland Stakes? Image obviously loved to be in front. However, the Derby was a six-teenth longer than the Ashland. Could Image handle the distance at such a grueling pace?

Or should she rate the filly and then make a move at the end? This was risky for many reasons—getting boxed in, clipped, or interfered with. Plus Image hated to have dirt kicked in her face, hated the jostling of the other horses, and hated to be behind.

Melanie worried her lip. Her palms sweated. She needed to decide.

Trust your instincts, she finally told herself. One ahead of her, Speed.com loaded smoothly. Melanie turned Image's head toward the chute and clucked.

Jumping forward, Image almost ran over the gate crew in her eagerness to load. Startled, the men scattered. Melanie was almost as surprised as they were. Image had reluctantly loaded for the Ashland Stakes. Should she take this as a good sign? "Good girl." Melanie stroked Image's neck. The filly's muscles were vibrating with excitement.

"One back!" one starter hollered as two others linked hands behind Gratis and propelled him into the chute.

Melanie lowered her goggles. The empty track stretched before them like a sunlit river. The crowd thundered like a rushing waterfall. Image's ears were tipped forward, and she seemed poised on tiptoe. If Melanie read Image's body language correctly, this was going to be a fast start. *And I'm ready.*

A hush fell over the crowd. Melanie ducked her head, the brim of her helmet touching Image's mane, and focused her attention inward. She needed another perfect break—like the one at the Ashland Stakes—to get away from Speed.com and Gratis. That meant she and Image had to leave the chute in harmony. She visualized the two of them leaping smoothly from the starting gate. Grabbing a hunk of mane, she crouched low on the filly's neck. As if in a dream, Melanie heard the bell ring. Then the front gates snapped open, Image leaped from the gate, and a roar filled Melanie's head.

Speed, Gratis, and Image broke simultaneously. The

two colts swerved toward Image as if threatening to smash her between them. Flattening her ears in anger, Image bounded forward with such an incredibly long stride, it felt as if she were jumping a wide chasm.

The huge effort propelled Image safely between the two colts. The thrust of the filly's hindquarters also shot Melanie onto her neck. She clutched mane, trying to keep her balance. At the same time, she tried to keep her head. They thundered past the clubhouse, Image running alone on the outside of the track. To her left, the first six horses were bunched in an uneven pack. Melanie caught sight of Wonder's Star smack in the middle; Celtic Mist was slightly ahead. Ingleside, who'd broken from the number one gate, was on the rail, leading by a length. Then Melanie lost track as Image began to fight her hold on the reins.

Something was up.

Melanie glanced right. Gratis was slowly gaining on the filly. The colt's nose was even with Melanie's right foot. She shot a look over her shoulder. Gratis's eye was hard, his nostrils red. Wolf was crouched low. The look in his eyes was as fierce as his mount's. As they galloped around the clubhouse turn, Melanie checked left. Speed.com was also dogging the filly. Turk Watson had his whip visible. He glared triumphantly at Melanie when he saw her glance his way. *Your filly's not going to be able to keep up that pace. Watch us catch you,* he seemed to be saying with his smirk.

Go ahead and try, Melanie thought grimly. The back-stretch loomed before them. Ingleside continued to hug the inside rail with a slight lead. Celtic Mist was right beside him. The rest of the field was still incredibly tight. With so many strong runners, no one wanted to get too far ahead or behind.

Melanie hunkered low. "Easy, easy," she crooned. Image needed to stay balanced for the homestretch turn. Since she was on the outside, she would be running a longer distance. It was better than being boxed in or shoved, but it also meant that the filly needed to conserve her strength for the final sprint to the finish line.

"Incredible, folks!" Melanie caught the announcer's words. "These colts—and the filly—are not giving up without a fight. Usually we see a fast pace horse. Usually several lose steam. But this field is running in a solid pack as they head for the homestretch turn."

With a tap of her heel, Melanie signaled Image to switch leads. The filly changed without a hitch. *Yes!* Image's breathing was deep and even. Flipping off her dusty goggles, Melanie took a quick look toward the rail. Her heart leaped into her throat. As they rounded the turn, Ingleside and Celtic Mist were slowly pulling ahead. Beside them, about a length behind, War Ghost, Derry O'Dell, TV Time, and Star were bunched together so tightly they were a blur of colors. Right beside Image, Speed.com galloped strongly. Melanie couldn't see

Gratis, but she could hear the colt's heavy breathing.

They were both gaining!

Don't panic. Image still has energy to spare. Melanie could feel it in the smooth power of her ground-eating stride. *You're still in a good position. Wait, wait.*

She pulled on clean goggles as they headed down the homestretch. *This is it. This is when heart and sheer determination kick in.* "You can do it, Image," Melanie murmured. Slowly, as the nine horses galloped down the homestretch, the field spread out. Ingleside gave out, and Celtic Mist took the lead on the rail. Speed.com faded, despite the cracks of Turk Watson's whip. Beside Image, Gratis, refusing to be bested, forged ahead. Melanie's heart began to race along with Image. "This is it, girl. Show them what you can do!"

One furlong to go. Crouching lower, Melanie made herself one with her horse. She used her body and hands to propel the filly faster, faster toward the invisible finish line. Silently she urged her on: *You can do it. You're the best. I've always known it. Give it everything, one more time.*

And just as Melanie knew she would, the filly responded. She flicked her ears once. Then Melanie felt her accelerate, felt the power flow through them as they soared down the track. She didn't need to look right or left. She knew they'd left the others behind. They were unstoppable. Unbeatable. "Perfect Image is taking the lead! Look at that filly go! A length! Two lengths! She's leaving the field behind! And the winner of the Kentucky Derby is number eight, Perfect Image, ridden by Melanie Graham. Folks, you just witnessed an incredible race!"

We won! Melanie wanted to scream the words to the whole world. Standing in her stirrups, she raised her whip to the sky as she slowed the filly to a canter. The roar of the crowd was like a thundering song.

Then Melanie heard another sound. A sound that sent a chill up her spine.

A quick, sharp sound like the snapping of a branch.

Or bone.

Then she felt a shift of balance. An uneven step.

And then Image went down.

13

Headfirst, Image plowed into the hard dirt track. Melanie kicked her feet from the stirrups. She tucked into a ball, reacting instinctively, so when she hit the ground, she somersaulted onto her shoulder and side.

Instantly she jumped to her feet. The eight horses, slowing after the finish, swerved erratically around her. Melanie darted around them, not caring if she was run over. *She had to get to Image!*

Down on one side, the filly was struggling to stand. "No, no!" Melanie cried. She'd heard the bone snap. She knew what would happen if Image stood up. She would try to run, to race after the other horses, to win again and again.

"No!" Tears flooded Melanie's eyes. She dove to the ground by the filly's head and draped her body over the horse's neck. "No, Image. You can't get up," she whispered, trying to keep the anguish, fear, and heartache from her voice. "Please, please, please."

Panic made her voice crack. Her pulse raced out of control. She chanced a look at Image's front legs. The left one was bent at an awkward angle below the knee. If it was broken and Image put weight on it, it would tear the tendons, flesh, and muscle.

"Hurry!" Melanie cried out. A second later the patrol car drove up, and the track vet, Dr. Hillman, jumped out. Then the horse ambulance and emergency vehicle drove onto the track. Image threw up her head, her eyes wild. Through her tears, Melanie began humming the melody of the Spanish song Marcos had sung to the filly.

Dr. Hillman ran over, a special inflatable support cast in his hand. "Can you keep her still?"

Melanie nodded. Marcos and Jazz appeared by her side. Crouching down, Marcos soothed the filly with words and soft strokes. Suddenly Image began flailing her legs. Her knee knocked Melanie hard in the ribs, and a flash of pain almost made her faint.

"Shh, my señorita," Marcos sang to Image. "Let the doctor do his work."

"The cast is on." Dr. Hillman bent down beside Melanie. "Now, this is the hardest part. We've got to get her up. As soon as she's standing, I'll give her a mild sedative. It's imperative we keep her mobile yet as quiet as possible."

Melanie nodded in understanding. She gritted her

teeth against the pain in her side. "I need to help you. She trusts me."

"That's fine," Dr. Hillman said. "Except we've done this many times." He smiled gently. "We're pretty good at it by now. Trust *us*. You can ride with her in the ambulance. It's equipped with a special sling."

"But I—" Melanie cut in. She needed to tell them that she couldn't leave Image. That it was all her fault the filly had broken down. If only she hadn't entered the Derby! If only she hadn't asked the filly for everything she had!

Because everything had been too much.

"You'll have to move," the horse ambulance attendant said. "We're going to try to get her up." In a daze, Melanie stared up at him. Putting his arm under hers, Jazz lifted her to her feet. She staggered and collapsed against him. "Jazz, it's all my fault. Image ran her heart out. But I asked for more."

He wrapped his arms around her and pressed her close. Melanie winced at the pain. "Melanie. Do *not* blame yourself. Image wanted to win as much as you."

"She wanted to win, yes, but she knew I wanted it more. She ran for me! She broke her leg for me!"

"We don't know it's broken yet," Jazz said, but Melanie could hear the doubt in his voice.

"I *know* it is," she said dully, her words muffled against his emerald-green tie, her tears staining Image's racing colors.

Melanie pulled away from Jazz. That's when she noticed the screens the track crew had placed around the scene of the accident. Screens to shield the crowd from the horror.

A bitter taste filled Melanie's mouth. She thought about all the Derby glamour—the festival fireworks, Pegasus Parade, steamboat race, mint juleps, endless parties, and blanket of roses. But this was part of horse racing, too.

The attendants and crew were circled around Image. Melanie couldn't see her. A scream of panic rose in her throat. What was happening? Then she heard the filly grunt with pain. "Jazz! They're hurting her!" Melanie tried to wrench away from him, but he held her arms.

"Melanie, they're—" But when he glimpsed her face, his words died.

Suddenly Melanie's head began to swim. Her breath came in gasps.

"She's in shock!" she heard Jazz call.

Then she blacked out.

Melanie opened her eyes, then quickly closed them against the bright bluish light. She groaned, instantly realizing where she was—the hospital.

"Mel?"

Melanie squinted. Will, Susan, and Ashleigh were

gazing down at her. Their eyes were bloodshot and puffy, as if they'd been crying.

Her dad looked the worst, as though he hadn't slept for a month.

"Hey, guys, what's going on?" Melanie rose up on her elbow and felt a shard of pain in her side. "Oh, man." She fell back against the pillow. "What in the world happened? Wasn't I just in here?"

Ashleigh nodded. "For that same rib, too. Only this time you had some bruising on your lung, so they're keeping you here for a couple of days to let it heal."

Melanie felt her side, which was taped with a wide bandage. "But I can't stay here." She frowned, trying to remember why. Then it hit her with such force that she forgot about the pain. "Image!" Bolting upright, she swung her legs from under the covers.

"Mel!" Will grabbed her shoulders "You're hooked to a dozen tubes. You have a broken rib. You *cannot* get up."

"But Image . . ." Melanie's eyes widened in horror. She stared into space, the details of the race playing in her head like a frightening movie. "Where is she? I have to be with her!"

Will and Ashleigh exchanged such anguished looks that tears began to stream down Melanie's cheeks. "No. No. Don't tell me. She . . . she *can't* be . . ."

"No, she's not dead," Ashleigh said. "She's at the

track hospital. Our vet is with Dr. Hillman. They've sedated her and X-rayed her leg. But Mel, I'm not going to lie. It doesn't look good."

Tears rolled down Melanie's cheeks. Picking up her legs, Will gently placed them back on the bed and pulled the covers over them and up to her chin. Ashleigh handed her a tissue.

"Tell me everything," Melanie whispered.

"She broke her cannon bone. Fortunately, due to your quick thinking, it was a clean break, without a lot of damage to the muscle and tissue."

Melanie nodded. "Go on."

"The vets are confident they can repair the break. There's new technology—metal implants that are strong enough to hold a horse's weight. And they have special slings—like the one we used with Raven—to help keep weight off the leg while it heals. However . . ."

Melanie closed her eyes. A tear leaked out and meandered down her cheek. Her father, still sitting beside her on the bed, took her hand and held it between his. "You don't need to tell me," Melanie whispered. She knew the problems. The bone would need at least three months to heal. For three months Image would have to be confined in a sling in a stall—sheer torture for a horse like Image.

"She's already fighting the sedatives," Ashleigh

said. "They barely got her X-rayed. The operation may take eight to ten hours. They're afraid that even if it is successful, when she wakes from the anesthesia, she'll only redamage the leg."

Melanie held her hand up. "You don't need to explain it to me." She glanced at her dad. "Where's Jazz?"

Will ran his fingers through his hair in a weary gesture. "The poor guy's trying to handle the media. It's been a zoo. He had to smile graciously and give a speech when he accepted the trophy at the ceremony after the race. The officials and commentators played down Image's injury. Not that I blame them. Puts a damper on the ratings to have the winning filly—"

"Dad, I don't want to hear any more." Pulling the covers over her face, Melanie slid down in the bed.

He patted her knee. "I don't blame you. The hospital has a security officer outside your door. There are reporters camped on the hospital lawn waiting to interview you, but we've told them no media allowed."

She pulled the sheet from her face. "How long do I have to stay here?"

"Until Monday," Ashleigh said. "They want to make sure your lung doesn't collapse."

"Will you tell Jazz I need to talk to him?"

Will nodded.

Ashleigh touched her hand. "There's one other person who really wants to talk to you—if you can handle it."

156

"Christina? Oh, gosh. I never even asked about the race! How'd she do?"

"Are you sure you want to know?" Will asked.

Melanie sighed. "I can't pretend the race didn't happen."

"Christina will tell you," Ashleigh said, and then she, Will, and Susan said good-bye. A few minutes later Christina peeked hesitantly around the door frame.

"Hey, Chris. How'd you and Star do?"

Christina grimaced as she came over to the bed. "Terrible." When she got closer, Melanie could see the dried tears on her cheeks.

"I want to hear every detail," Melanie demanded. "I *need* to hear every detail."

Christina sat awkwardly on the edge of the bed. "We got boxed in behind TV Time, War Ghost, and Derry O'Dell. I kept thinking one of them would fade and we could move up. Star had plenty of oomph. But they kept on plugging, and we never found a hole." She shrugged. "I guess it just wasn't meant to be. Gratis got third, did you hear? Cindy and Ben are really excited. They're already talking about the Preakness."

Melanie clutched Christina's hand. "And you?"

"Come on, we were almost last over the finish line."

"Chris, it was a tight field. You said Star had plenty

of energy left. Your only mistake was strategy. That's all the more reason to go for it!"

Christina looked down at her hands. "I'll think about it. Of course, Celtic Mist got second." She made a face.

"Was Brad mad that Image won?"

Christina thought a second. "Actually, he was pretty subdued. I think the accident—" Suddenly tears started pouring from her eyes. "Oh, Mel. I am *so* sorry about Image. *Everybody's* sorry. I mean, as much as we know the risks, it's still such a horrible shock when it happens, especially to a horse—and a person—you know and love."

Melanie stifled her own tears. "Look, Chris, I can't talk about it right now. I—I—"

Leaning forward, Christina gave her a quick hug. "I just wanted to let you know that you're my best friend, Mel, and I love you, and I want to help in any way I can."

"I know. And I'm sorry about all that happened before the race. You know, you were right. I did run away from Whitebrook without talking to you. And that wasn't fair of me. But right now—" Melanie squeezed her eyes shut, trying to hold back a wave of sadness. "Right now I need to talk to Jazz," she finally choked out. "Can you try to find him?"

"Of course." Christina hugged her one last time before leaving.

With a miserable sigh, Melanie settled back onto the pillow. Part of her wished she could go to Image. But part of her didn't. She didn't want to face the onslaught of reporters. And she didn't want to see her beautiful, wild, impetuous filly sedated and strapped onto an operating table.

Before the race, Melanie had planned for every angle. She'd even worried about Image injuring herself. But she'd never once thought that Image might break a leg or have a catastrophic accident. The reporter, Brice Workman, had called her naive, a kid.

He was right. She thought back to when she lived in New York City. Then her foolishness had caused a horrible accident with a different horse. And now, even though she was older, she was once again responsible for a tragedy. A tragedy that couldn't possibly have a happy ending.

Just then she saw a pair of legs topped by an enormous bouquet of roses walk into the room. "Hey." Jazz peered around the flowers, a sad, exhausted smile on his face, and Melanie burst into tears.

Setting the roses on the bedside table, Jazz sat on the bed and put his arms around her. "Wow, I've had fans swoon, but I've never had one burst into tears before," he joked weakly.

"Sorry. Can you get me a tissue?" she sniffled.

He pulled a linen handkerchief from his pants pocket. She blew her nose loudly. "I'll be okay in a minute."

"Go ahead and cry."

"No, I've got to stop. We've got to talk about Image."

Jazz's face turned white. Standing abruptly, he picked up the roses. "Do you think the nurses have a vase?"

Melanie's tears instantly dried. She caught his hand and tugged him closer. "Jazz, tell me what's going on."

Slowly he sat back down. His green tie was crooked, his white shirt stained. Deep circles underlined his dark eyes. Melanie had never seen him look so defeated.

"Image is having a reaction to the sedation. She's fighting everything the vets do. She's already torn the inflatable cast. She's whacked her leg until it's bleeding. Right now they've got it under control, but there are concerns that the anesthesia won't work if they try to operate. And then there's the problem with recovery. When a horse comes out of the anesthesia, it usually thrashes around and often—"

Melanie put one finger on his lips. "Don't say any more," she whispered. "I've heard enough. It doesn't matter if they successfully operate and stabilize the leg with whatever high-tech gadgets they have. If Image is fighting now, what will she be like when she comes out of the anesthesia? She'll be wild. And then there's the three months of recovery time. She'd have to stay

160

confined and absolutely quiet for the leg to heal. And you know Image, Jazz—she would *never* survive being confined."

Turning sideways, Jazz held both her hands in his. "Melanie, we have to try."

Melanie's lower lip began to tremble, but she forced herself to continue, to make the hardest decision she'd ever made. "Jazz, I truly believe that Image would rather die than be locked up day after day, hung from the ceiling like a slab of meat. Freedom is more important to her than, well, *life*."

Now tears were streaming down Jazz's cheeks. Silently he nodded.

"You know how much I love Image," Melanie continued, her voice quivering, tears running down her face. "I love her so much, I'm willing to break my own heart to save hers. You have to tell the vets, Jazz. No matter what people say, you have to tell them our decision. Let them know it's *not* that we're giving up. We're letting her go."

14

"CLIMB IN CAREFULLY, DEAR," THE NURSE SAID MONDAY morning as she guided Melanie into the wheelchair. Christina hovered around them both. Already she and Susan had helped Melanie shower and pack her few things. "You're such a tiny bird," the nurse added. "I'd hate for you to fall."

"It's just my rib," Melanie protested as she settled into the chair for the ride down to the car.

"Rib today, leg tomorrow," the nurse said matter-of-factly. "That's what we say when you jockeys come into the emergency room."

Christina and Melanie laughed, although it was more true than funny.

"Ready?" Susan poked her head into the room.

"You're all checked out, Melanie. Will and Jazz are waiting in the car. Hospital security let us park at a back entrance so we can whisk you out without the media knowing."

Melanie made a disgusted noise. "Don't they have anything better to do?"

"You and Image are hot news," Christina said.

Image. Melanie pressed her hand against the ache in her heart. How long would it be before the mention of her name didn't hurt? Years?

No, it would *always* hurt. Wasn't Ashleigh still grieving for Wonder?

As the nurse wheeled her down the hall, Melanie fell into a deep gloom. In some ways being in the hospital had protected her from the reality of her decision. The past two nights, the nurse had given her a double-strength sleeping pill. The day before, she'd had a million visitors. And that morning, hospital routine and preparations for leaving had occupied her mind.

But now she was going back to Whitebrook. Every day she'd have to look at Image's empty paddock. Every day she'd have to ask herself the same question: Had she made the right decision? And every day she'd have to live with what she'd done.

As they went down in the elevator, Christina chattered nonstop, as if afraid that they'd all start crying if she stopped talking. Even Susan chimed in cheerfully with tidbits about well-wishers who had called or sent flowers.

When they finally reached the ground floor and Melanie spotted Jazz, she breathed a sigh of relief. "Will's waiting outside in the car," Jazz said when the nurse pushed the wheelchair from the elevator. "We've got to make it fast. There are several reporters snooping around."

"That's crazy. It's not like I'm some famous actress."

"No, you're some famous jockey," Jazz said. Walking ahead, he pushed open the double doors. Will had pulled a rental car up to the curb. The back door was open. As soon as they reached the sidewalk, Melanie stood up, thanked the nurse, and ducked into the backseat of the car. Christina and Jazz slid into the back as well, and Susan climbed in the front seat.

"How's my favorite girl?" Will asked.

Melanie tried to smile. "Too tired to talk. If that's okay with everybody."

The drive took about an hour. When they reached the Lexington area, Melanie realized they weren't heading to Whitebrook. "Where are we going?"

"Nobody told you?" Will said.

"Told me what?" Melanie narrowed her eyes.

Jazz leaned forward to look around Christina. "We're all staying at Townsend Acres for a few days. In the cottage. Brad suggested it, and he's right. The security will keep out unwanted busybodies. At some point, Mel, you're going to have to talk to reporters. But this way we can do it on our own terms."

"That does make sense. But—" She looked worriedly at Christina. Did they just not want her back at Whitebrook?

Christina grinned. "I'll be staying with you, too. I've got my bags packed and in the trunk." Melanie felt immense relief.

Susan turned to look into the backseat. "Your dad and I can stay until Wednesday."

"I can stay until then, too," Jazz said.

"Parker's offered to take us to school," Christina added. "So it should be cool. Like a big slumber party. Believe me, I need a little partying myself."

Minutes later Will turned into Townsend Acres' drive. The guards waved him ahead. *It's just as well we're staying here for a while,* Melanie thought as they cruised down the manicured, tree-lined drive. *I won't be faced with as many memories.*

When they drove past the training barn, Jazz suddenly sat up. "Will, you need to stop here a minute." He pointed to the Townsend Horse Center.

"What for?" Melanie frowned, instantly alert.

"You have to sign some forms," he explained. "Dr. Hillman left them here for you."

"Oh." Reluctantly Melanie climbed from the car.

She joined Jazz and they went into the medical facility. Brad was standing inside the modern office talking to a gentleman wearing a lab coat.

"Melanie!" he greeted enthusiastically. "I'm glad to see you're out of the hospital. How's the busted rib?"

"Fine." Automatically she rubbed it through her shirt. "Jazz said I needed to sign some forms."

"Right, right. But first, have you met Dr. Dalton? He's my full-time vet. Finest in the country."

Plastering on a smile, Melanie shook the man's hand. "Nice meeting you."

"Nice meeting you, Ms. Graham."

Melanie noticed how no one mentioned the Derby. It was as if she and Image had never raced. Or won.

"Before you go, how about a tour of our medical center?" Taking her arm, Brad propelled her toward a closed door.

"Um, I—" Melanie shot Jazz an anxious look that said, *Save me!* But he was talking to Dr. Dalton, his back to her.

"When I built the center, I wanted the best," Brad explained as he hurried her down a hall. "Best surgical unit, best doctors, best equipment to serve the best horses in Kentucky."

Melanie forced a smile. "You do strive for the best."

He flashed her his brightest smile. "Couldn't have said it better myself." He opened a door and waved her in. "But what I was really aiming for was the best facility to treat injured racehorses. That meant experimenting with new technology. I thought you, of all people, would understand how important this is."

"You're right. I do," Melanie said sincerely. "I'm just sorry there wasn't something we could do for—"

The name caught in her throat. Melanie choked back the tears. She did *not* want to break down in front of this man. Ducking her head, she hurried through the door. Instantly she was hit with warm, steamy air.

"I wanted to show you my therapeutic pool," Brad said. "We're using it to successfully treat all kinds of injuries. Yesterday we tried out something new."

"That's really nice," Melanie murmured.

Putting his hands on her shoulders, Brad steered her to the side of the huge pool. Two ramps covered with rubber led into the pool. Cables hung from the ceiling. They were attached to a horse that was swimming away from Melanie. A black horse. Her nose, with a snippet of white, just broke the surface of the water.

Melanie gasped. Her legs buckled, and she fell to her knees. *It was Image.*

"Wh-Wha—?" Melanie stammered.

Brad leaned over. "You're not imagining things, Melanie. It's Image. And she's doing great."

Melanie still didn't understand.

Suddenly Jazz was beside her, too. Crouching next to her, he took her hand. "I know what you told me,

Melanie, and I'm sorry to go against your wishes. But I wasn't quite ready to let Image go. Only I didn't know what to do. Then Brad came to the rescue."

They both glanced up, but Brad was gone. "He suggested we bring Image here. He wanted to try his new setup." Jazz pointed to the cables. "They operated on Image right by the side of the pool. But first they put her in a special horse-sized wet suit. They repaired her leg—I'll let Dr. Dalton explain to you in detail what they did—then raised her upright. As soon as she started to come out of the anesthesia, they lowered her into the pool."

Still in shock, Melanie could only stare at Jazz before turning back to watch Image. The filly was dog-paddling at the other end, treading water horse style. Two attendants stood on the sidelines, watching her every move. "Into the *pool?*" she finally repeated, still not believing what she was seeing.

"I know it sounds wild. But when Brad explained it to me, I also knew it was worth a try. Usually a horse exerts about six hundred pounds of force on a front leg. Right after recovery, when the horse first comes out of the anesthesia and tries to stand up or thrashes around, it exerts about *three thousand* pounds. That's why they use a sling to support the horse afterward. However, we knew that wouldn't work with Image.

"Dr. Dalton and his team devised a sling that was also a wet suit," Jazz went on. "The horse is lowered into the water. When it comes out of the anesthesia and thrashes around, there is no force on the leg at all!"

As Melanie listened her heart began to beat faster. "And it worked?"

"Totally. Just like we thought, when Image woke up, she went crazy. But the attendants were able to keep her confined to the deep water. After about half an hour, she regained total consciousness. It took her a while to calm down, but her leg withstood the strain. Then they made her swim half an hour longer—until she was tired. The implant the orthopedic surgeon put in her leg is designed to support a thousand pounds. That means Image can be hand-walked as often as needed. She's kept in a huge, airy stall right outside the pool. Baby's stabled with her. Marcos has agreed to be with her twenty-four hours a day. And she can swim anytime she wants, every day, until she's exhausted."

He swung around to face her. "Melanie, I know it's not perfect. I know it will still be hard on Image. And there's always a chance of infection or problems with the implants. But I still had to try."

Melanie bit back the tears. "But Jazz, you realize that no matter how successful the operation, she'll never race again."

"Hey, that wasn't even a consideration. You and Image are too important to me."

Melanie's tears overflowed. "Thank you, Jazz," she choked out. "I know that's not enough, but—"

Jazz kissed her softly, stopping her words. Then he stood up, bringing her with him. "Melanie, I want you to know, I'm in this for the long haul. It's you, Image, and me. If you'll have me," he added almost shyly.

"I guess I don't have any choice," she teased, happier than she'd ever been. "Thank you for everything."

"Thank *Brad*," he said. "Wherever he went."

"Oh, I will. But first . . ." Grinning, Melanie pulled away from Jazz and kicked off her shoes. "I need to thank *Image*."

"Wait," Jazz said in alarm. "You can't go in there with her. That's a pool for horses. You have a busted rib!"

"And I don't care!" Joy filled Melanie's chest until it spilled over, and she began to laugh hysterically. "That's my horse in there!" she added. Holding her nose, she jumped into the pool. As she swam toward Image, she called out her name. The filly pricked her ears, began to turn in the water, then saw Melanie. She whinnied, and bubbles burst from her nostrils and mouth. Melanie's tears mingled with the warm pool water. She needed to say so much to Image. She needed to apologize for being wrong. She needed to thank her for being a special horse, for having the will to survive, and for having given everything she had— even when it had almost cost her her life.

Alice Leonhardt has been horse-crazy since she was five years old. Her first pony was a pinto named Ted. When she got older, she joined Pony Club and rode in shows and rallies. Now she just rides her Quarter Horse, April, for fun. The author of more than thirty books for children, she still finds time to take care of two horses, two cats, two dogs, and two children, as well as teach at a community college.